DEEP SLEEPER

DETECTIVE PAUL CULLEN MYSTERIES BOOK 4

PAUL PILKINGTON

First published 2023

Published by Fast Paced Fiction

Paperback ISBN: 978-1-915367-30-3

This novel is written in British (UK) English. British English words, spelling (favourite, colour, etc.) and grammar are used throughout.

Cover design by Jeanine Henning.

For all my readers, and particularly those thousand of you who pre-ordered this novel. I really appreciate your support - having readers is what makes writing worthwhile, so you are key to everything I do!

Deep Sleeper is about to depart.

I hope you enjoy the ride.

ALSO BY PAUL PILKINGTON

Detective Paul Cullen Mysteries:

Long Gone

Fallen Angel

Dead Ahead

Deep Sleeper

May Day (coming 2024)

Emma Holden Trilogy:

The One You Love

The One You Fear

The One You Trust

Standalone Novels:

Someone to Save You

I Heard You

For Your Own Protection

PART I

1

Previously

In the Midwestern town of Hope, Kansas, Curtis Chesterfield skipped through the channels, thirty or more, as he sat in the dark living room. There was nothing on the television anymore. Unless you wanted to watch reality TV. He settled for an action movie, all explosions and car chases. He'd seen the movie a number of times, but even at a quarter past midnight he didn't yet want to retire to bed, given his recent struggles with insomnia.

He would persevere with this second rate entertainment, until he felt himself falling asleep. Then he would hurry to bed (he was already in his pyjamas and had brushed his teeth), slip in under the covers next to his wife of forty years, Cindy, and pray for sleep to envelop him.

The doctor would surely prescribe medication, sleeping tablets, to help him on his way. But Curtis has resisted visiting and telling Dr Murdoch his troubles, because this town was small and, being the Mayor, he wanted to keep his personal life out of any spotlight.

It wasn't that he distrusted the doctor, but there was the receptionist, the newly appointed practice nurse, and what about all those fellow townsfolk who happened to be in the waiting room?

Instead he'd ordered some herbal pills from the internet. According to the advert they were effective at treating a range of sleep disorders. Although Curtis knew that his nocturnal difficulties were merely the symptom of something which was much more difficult to deal with.

And of the real problem, he could certainly not tell anyone.

His life would be over.

He was dozing when the noise jolted him awake.

Must have been the TV.

But the movie had finished and had been replaced by a talkshow.

In his dreams then...

He cursed his luck that he'd actually managed to fall asleep, but just in the wrong place. In his half-woken state, he decided to grasp onto the opportunity that had been presented to him, and lay flat across the sofa, jabbing the remote control to kill the television. Maybe he would fall back asleep here, rather than ascend to the bedroom and risk waking up properly. He pulled one of Cindy's knitted throws across him and closed his eyes.

Boom!

'What the hell?'

That came from outside, surely. He jumped up from the sofa, and hurried towards the window, pulling back the curtains. There seemed to be a light coming from somewhere nearby.

Boom!

Not as loud as last time, but still extremely worrying. Without thinking about his state of dress, or any possible safety implications, Curtis headed for the door, scrambling for his shoes and grabbing a coat as he left the house.

As he raced out towards the light, just around the corner of their street, he came face to face with Max Thornton, his neighbour and childhood friend of over sixty years.

'It's coming from the rail track,' Max gasped, resting his hands on his hips as he caught his breath. 'Big explosions.'

'Train crash?' Curtis said, horrified. The town of Hope in Kansas was right next to one of the major trans-american railroad routes, linking east to west. The railroad was the reason the town had come into being, just over a hundred years ago. It was perfectly positioned as a freight stop for refuelling as the two-mile-long freight trains rolled across the country.

'I think it's happened again,' Max replied.

The last accident had been over fifty years ago, when a ruptured fuel tank exploded and blew a waiting freight train sky high, killing the driver and three local workers.

One of them was Curtis's grandfather.

Shortly after that, the refuelling facilities were removed - substituted for more modern, safer facilities further down the line - leaving Hope as just another midwest town along those thousands upon thousands of miles of track.

They both hurried around the corner as Curtis ignored the shooting pain from his troublesome right knee. Dogs were barking and lights started to pop on in the houses as the residents stirred from their slumber. Some were now at their top windows, looking out anxiously.

'Dear God,' Curtis cried, as they rounded the bend towards the rail track, just a hundred metres away from the town boundary. It was a scene of utter devastation. A freight train had derailed, with the front portion laying on its side. The engine itself looked undamaged, but the containers behind it were already ablaze and thick, black smoke was billowing from them, sending great plumes skyward.

It was only then that Curtis registered the smell.

'Chemicals,' Max said, sensing the same. 'Cover your face!'

The two men pulled their t-shirts up towards their nose and Curtis held his coat against his mouth. They stopped there for a few seconds, before Curtis again sprung into action.

'The driver,' he said, setting off towards the trackside.

'Curtis! No, it's too dangerous!' Max shouted behind him, but he was undeterred, and, with his knee now really disagreeing, hobbled onward. He was the Mayor of this town, and the first on the scene. He had a duty to try and help. Fifty years earlier, brave residents had tried to save his grandfather and those other men, and he would do the same.

'Curtis! Damn it!' Max screamed, his voice now distant. 'You'll get yourself killed.'

As Curtis neared the train, the intense, chemical-fuelled heat radiated towards him like a moving wall. And the smell was so strong, it was burning his throat like cheap whiskey. Max was right - this was a suicide mission - there was no way he would be able to do anything, even if the driver and any other workers had survived the initial crash and explosions.

It was just too hot and the chemicals too acrid.

He had to stop.

But his body didn't have chance to catch up with his mind, and he was still moving forwards when the fireball engulfed the locomotive. The shockwave blasted Curtis backwards and he left the ground for several seconds, slamming down hard on the road.

The last thing he remembered was thinking that he finally could get some decent rest.

2

Present Day

'ARE YOU SURE YOU'RE ALRIGHT?' Cullen asked, gazing anxiously at his former colleague. Tony Beswick, until recently a Detective Sergeant in the British Transport Police, was looking up in awe (or was that terror?) at the imposing structure of the London Eye with what appeared to be a tear in his eye.

'I'm fine, Boss,' he said, rather unconvincingly, pinching the bridge of his nose dry. 'Just getting myself ready for the ride, mentally, you know.'

Unfortunately, Cullen did know...

'You look like you're about to face the executioner,' Cullen quipped.

Tellingly, Tony didn't crack a smile.

Cullen watched on as his friend continued with his death-row stare at the slowly-turning, huge wheel. 'I don't want you having another heart attack - especially not at the top of that thing.'

'Don't,' Tony said. He thought on something, now looking even more anxious. 'Do you think they have defibrillators in every pod? You know, in case something happens?'

'I wouldn't bet on it. Too expensive.'

Tony frowned, perturbed. 'No, I guess not.'

Cullen felt bad as it looked like Tony was having second thoughts. It had been Cullen's role to help his vertigo-suffering friend through this latest bucket-list challenge, not to put him off.

But still, he really didn't want him having a coronary at over one hundred metres in the air, trapped inside a transparent pod with a bunch of random tourists, suspended above the Thames.

It had been several months since an off-duty Tony Beswick had collapsed on Oxford Street, in pursuit of a bag snatcher. Emergency surgery had saved his life, fitting a series of stents to re-open his blocked arteries, but it had been touch and go for a time. The heart scare had brought forward his retirement plans, with Cullen's long-time partner taking the opportunity to leave the force and enjoy a well-earned rest.

Except, to Cullen's surprise, Tony's near death experience had prompted something of a character shift. Previously a self-defined "unadventurous" individual, Tony had drawn up a bucket list of challenges that he wanted to take on over the coming year.

Last week the life-long arachnophobe had handled a tarantula at London Zoo.

The previous month the shy introvert had given an entertaining and genuinely funny after-dinner talk at a police officers' retirement event, down at City Hall in front of the Mayor and Chief Constable.

Cullen had been genuinely impressed, particularly when Tony had confided in him just how nervous he had been.

Cullen decided to give him one last way out, given that they were almost at the front of the queue.

'It's okay if you've changed your mind,' he said, putting a hand on Tony's shoulder. 'It's totally okay. You can just move on to the next challenge. You don't have to prove anything to anyone.'

'Stop, you're worrying me,' Tony said.

'Pardon?'

'You're talking like a therapist.'

Cullen laughed. 'You've never been to a therapist. Have you?'

'Saw them on TV.'

Cullen held up his hands in mock surrender and smiled. 'I'm just here for you, Tony, whatever you decide to do.'

'There you go again, Boss. Please stop it.' Tony looked up again at the wheel, and gathered himself. 'I'm fine,' he told himself. 'This will be fine. I'm fine.'

'Fine,' Cullen repeated. 'As long as you're happy.'

'I wouldn't go that far,' Tony replied in all seriousness. 'Maybe once the pod is over that top bit.'

Cullen had to agree.

'I really appreciate you doing this,' Tony added. 'I know you're not the biggest fan of heights either, which is why I asked you. I wanted someone who could empathise.'

'Happy to help. Sort of,' Cullen only half-joked. It was true, he wasn't great with heights, although he had nothing like the aversion that Tony Beswick suffered. 'Sit in the centre of the pod; there's a bench in the middle,' Cullen recommended.

'You've done your research?'

'Made use of it when I went on it with Sarah,' he admitted.

'Oh, I didn't know you'd been on it before.' Tony looked disappointed that this wasn't going to be a shared first experience.

'It was a few years ago, maybe ten?' Cullen wondered.

But the memories were strong. He'd hated that first half of the ride, as the pod moved ever-so-slowly towards the apex of the wheel.

'You'll particularly enjoy the second half of the ride,' Cullen said. Last time, it was only as it had begun to descend that he'd started to relax and had actually enjoyed the view. 'I promise.'

'Thanks, Boss,' Tony said. 'Like I said, I do appreciate you coming with me. I'm ready.'

'Let's do this, then,' Cullen said, as much to himself as his friend.

~

'ARE YOU OKAY, BOSS?'

Paul stared down at the floor of the pod.

'I'm fine,' he replied, keeping his head stock-still and refraining from looking at Tony. His heart was hammering against his chest, and his throat felt tight. 'Just needed a sit down, that's all.'

They were three quarters of the way up the first half of the revolution of the London Eye, which meant that the worst was to come. He'd been absolutely fine during the early stages of the climb, and had actually been enjoying the view across the Thames and Central London. But at the turn of an angle Cullen had suddenly wobbled, the ground beneath his feet seeming to shift worryingly, and he retreated to the central seating area for respite.

Tony put a hand on his shoulder. 'Just take it easy. We'll be over the top soon.'

Over the top...

Please, let it be over!

Cullen nodded, sweat beading on his brow. He felt ridiculous, a six foot three inch former rugby player, sitting here on the bench of shame, alongside the other panicked people. Of course, he'd found it difficult last time with Sarah, but he'd hoped the second time around on the wheel would be easier, not worse.

He ventured to raise his head and looked across to his friend, who had moved back over to the edge of the pod, hands on its transparent surface as he gazed out.

Tony turned around, seeming to sense that he was being observed, and beamed back at Cullen with the excitement of a toddler.

In a spectacular role reversal, Tony appeared to be having the time of his life.

At least that was something.

Cullen's pride got the better of him, so taking some steadying breaths, he attempted to stand, just as the pod was reaching the very top of the wheel. Muttering expletives, he took slow baby steps towards Tony, as if he was walking the plank of a pirate ship on a journey to the abyss.

'Get a grip, Paul,' he said to himself. 'You can do this.'

And he did do it, reaching Tony just as the wheel reached its apex.

'It's just amazing,' Tony said to Cullen who was now at his shoulder.

'An amazing view,' Cullen agreed, now finding the mid-air equivalent of his sea-legs.

'I didn't mean the view,' Tony replied. 'I meant the city - the greatest, most beautiful city in the world.'

'Agreed,' Cullen nodded, gazing out across the panorama of London's built environment; shaped over hundreds of years by the teeming mass of people who lived and moved there.

A city which plague, fire and bombs had ravaged but not defeated.

Recent years had seen an explosion of new, gleaming, high-rise buildings with modern names such as The Shard and The Walkie Talkie, that co-existed with the old - St. Paul's cathedral, St. Stephen's Tower and Big Ben, the Tower of London, and neighbouring Tower Bridge.

And then there was the busy world below - the underground network with its thousands of miles of track, screeching trains ghosting through blackened tunnels and millions of passengers; non-stop movement from morning until night. It was where a lot of life in London happened, including criminal behaviour. Cullen's role might have been national, leading the investigation of crimes across the UK rail network as Head of the British Transport Police's Major and Serious Organised Crime Unit, but a disproportionate amount of time was spent on investigations across Central London, and involving the London tube network in particular.

The danger and problems of the capital brought excitement and job satisfaction like he had never known.

It was a city and a job that Cullen had fallen in love with.

Which made his current predicament all the more difficult.

'Tony...'

'Yes, Boss?'

He nearly told Tony Beswick there and then what had been weighing heavily on his mind, but now was not the time...

'Nothing...'

Tony frowned but didn't push his friend.

Cullen's fear of heights had disappeared during this thoughts about the future, and he was now finally able to enjoy the ride.

He gazed at the hazy horizon, allowing himself to think about the future.

He would tell Tony today.

Once he had worked out what to say.

3

Previously

HOPE TOWN HALL was packed to the rafters for the emergency meeting. It was three weeks to the day since the derailment had led to the night-time evacuation of the town's two thousand residents, after chemicals being carried by the train were released into the environment to prevent an explosion that could have destroyed the town and sent a toxic cloud across most of the State.

Residents had been allowed back after a week, when the authorities had concluded that it was safe. But the local people were far from convinced. Many had suffered acute effects of the disaster - most commonly stinging eyes, sore throats and breathing issues. But once they returned, others complained of more insidious health problems that they attributed to the chemicals that had mostly sunk into the soil, but were also still visible on the surface in places.

And then there was a lingering smell, like some medieval

miasma, that permeated through the town and into the homes, lives and lungs of the people.

'As you know,' the official on the stage from the US Environmental Protection Agency began, 'since the incident we have carried out a range of in-depth tests. We would not have allowed you to return to your homes unless we had deemed it to be safe.'

A few shouts challenged his ascertain, and the general noise level rose, as Curtis looked on from his stage-side wheelchair.

The damage wasn't permanent, but the chair was needed for now. He had a badly bruised hip, swollen knees, and back spasms.

'A few weeks off your feet will work wonders,' the doctor had said, after they had concluded their investigations to rule out anything more serious.

'Of course,' the official continued, 'we will continue to monitor for any possible long-term environmental and health impacts. But as far as we can tell, there is no risk.'

'As far as you know,' came a voice from the side of the stage.

The official turned towards the man, but said nothing. He returned to address the residents. 'We will keep you informed of our ongoing investigations.'

He left the stage to a smattering of polite applause, which had been forced on the reticent audience by Curtis leading the claps. He might have his doubts about the authorities' claims, but that was no reason to be impolite to their guest.

The next slot would be uncomfortable enough for the poor guy.

Curtis brought the microphone to his mouth, shifting in the chair as his back complained. 'Thank you to Dr Peters.

And now we're going to hear from Professor Ben Brody, who is an independent environmental consultant, also very kindly looking into this for us. Professor Brody, the floor is yours.'

'Thank you, Curtis,' the man who had interrupted the official said confidently, as he took to the stage. The white-bearded former academic, in his mid sixties and with a reputation of being quite a maverick, had a track record in holding companies to account in the aftermath of similar incidents. He'd come highly recommended by the Mayor of Grangetown in Nebraska, where they had fought an oil company and won after a pipeline leak had polluted their groundwater, killing their livestock and ruining crop yields, possibly forever.

Ben Brody bounded up the steps and skipped onto the middle of the stage to begin his presentation, like a coiled spring released. The guy was short in stature, but made up for it in his louder than life personality. He wasn't afraid of saying controversial things and taking on big interests, no matter how uncomfortable. Curtis already knew what he was going to say, and was still nervous about the reaction among his fellow townsfolk. It was certainly a high stakes strategy, to let Professor Brody loose in this way, but they had up until now zero joy from Deep Distribution, the rail freight company that was responsible.

The company hadn't answered Curtis's emails or returned his numerous phone calls.

And the public statement was professional and curt, with no real recognition of what the residents had, and were still going through, or acknowledgment of either liability or ethical responsibility.

Their owner, the billionaire Daniel Deep, had been completely silent.

Nothing, either on official channels or social media.

That above everything had angered Curtis. The guy was busy tweeting about baseball and television shows, but hadn't had the decency in those long three weeks to address the human and environmental catastrophe that had blighted Curtis's beloved town and its people.

This was the start of the fight back.

There was a heavy press presence in the audience, invited by Curtis. Mostly regional, but also a couple of nationals too.

Word would certainly get around.

Just like it did in Grangetown.

'Let Daniel Deep ignore this,' Curtis muttered, as Professor Brody eyed the audience and prepared to tell all.

4

Present Day

'You sure you can spare the time?' Tony checked again, as they emerged from the tube and headed towards Leicester Square and the *Underground* bar.

'I've done my fair share of extra hours recently', Cullen replied, 'and everyone knows how to find me if something kicks off.'

Tony nodded. He knew about the current work situation at BTP Headquarters and just how crazy things had been. Despite having retired, Cullen had kept in close touch with his friend who remained interested in the goings-on at HQ.

They crossed the busy square, dodging slow moving, sight-seeing tourists from all corners of the globe, and headed down the much quieter side street towards the transport-themed bar.

It had been over six months since Cullen had visited the place - when he'd brought the young journalist Zack Carter there during the Natalie Long investigation. But at one time the Underground had been a weekly haunt after their shift on a Friday evening. In those early days, Tony - even though he was the junior officer in rank - had taken Cullen under his wings and made him feel not only at ease, but also part of the family.

'How long since you've been here?' Cullen asked, as they reached the door.

'Too long,' Tony smiled. 'I expect it's changed a lot,' he joked.

'Oh yes,' Cullen replied, grabbing hold of the handle and entering. 'That disco ball and dance floor they've fitted really makes a difference.'

They entered the venue, with its framed London Underground posters on the walls, and old tube station sign over the bar. The decor was exactly the same as it was when Cullen had first visited those years ago, and unchanged from Tony's early days of over a decade earlier.

That was its charm. Used by workers across London's transport network - train and bus drivers, engineers, and yes, transport police colleagues - to unwind at the end of long and often filthy days.

'Goodness, it's quiet in here,' Tony stated, as they emerged into the main area. It was practically deserted, save for a couple of older workers off in the corner, nursing pints.

'Very,' Cullen agreed. The place had seen a drop off in custom recently as younger workers chose not to carry on tradition. Nowadays it seemed almost more of a museum piece than a viable drinking establishment. Indeed, it only survived through a generous ex-railway engineer who had got lucky with the lottery a few years ago before leaving money to the place in his Will.

Even though Cullen was no longer a regular, it remained a place of good memories and comfort.

'Tony!' the long-time barman Mickey sang out when he saw the two approach. He was absolutely beaming. 'Really great to see you - really, really great!' He thrust out a thick, tattooed arm and they exchanged a vigorous but friendly shake.

'Good to see you too, Mickey,' Tony replied, actually blushing at the extreme reaction his appearance had provoked.

'So,' the barman said, 'enjoying retirement? I heard via the grapevine you'd gone out to pasture.'

Cullen saw something flash across Tony's face - discomfort maybe. He was feeling awkward, maybe. Even embarrassed?

Tony nodded. 'Yes, didn't have much choice really,' he said, still looking a little out of sorts. He patted at his chest. 'My ticker called time on my career.'

Cullen took another glance at his friend.

He looked sad.

Very different to earlier and how his face lit up with delight on the London Eye.

'Well, when you've got to go, you've got to go, as my wife said before she threw me out!' Mickey joked. 'So, can I get you the usual? It's on the house.'

They ordered and took their places in their usual, favourite bench seat. It was habit - they'd sat there the first time Cullen had visited, and not once deviated in the time since. Tucked away slightly from everyone else, it offered a vantage across the seating area. Cullen liked to keep half an eye out for things, even in a police-friendly venue such as this.

'So, Tony, what's up?' Cullen said, looking carefully at his former police partner. 'You look...deflated all of a sudden. Was it something that Mickey said?'

Tony tried to wave it away. 'Oh, it's nothing Boss.' But he was so unconvincing in his denials that Cullen sensed that Tony did really want to talk about what was bothering him.

'Spit it out, Tony,' he probed. 'What's up?'

Tony smiled sadly. 'Okay, okay.' He took a moment to try and compose himself, before shaking his head. 'I really miss the job,' he said, visibly upset all of a sudden. 'I *really* miss it.' He looked at Paul, his eyes watery. 'Come on, tell me I'm a daft sod and I should just move on with my life.'

Cullen smiled kindly. 'You know I would never do that. You loved your job, and it's a lot to lose, I understand,' he said, his own situation playing a large part in his response.

Tony thought on that response, scratching at his scalp through thinning hair. 'I actually dream about it, you know,' he admitted, with a chuckle. 'Not every night, but a lot of nights, I dream we're out there, investigating crimes. Last night, we were investigating the disappearance of the Flying Scotsman.'

Cullen laughed. 'Wow, now that is a high profile case. Did we find it?'

'Woke up before it had been resolved,' Tony revealed, with some disappointment. 'But last week we did catch a serial killer who was targeting people on the Elizabeth Line.'

'Of course...'

Tony settled into contemplative silence.

'It's normal,' Cullen assured him. 'You had a long career, and it meant a lot to you. You put your heart and soul into it. Surely it would be weirder, and more sad, if you could walk away and just forget about it, like none of it mattered?'

Tony nodded at that. 'I wasn't ready,' he stated. 'I thought I was, but I wasn't. Brenda had been on at me for a few years, trying to get me to retire, but I'd resisted it, Paul. I didn't want to leave. And then I had no choice.' He patted his chest again. 'I know it was the right thing to do - the sensible thing - but it doesn't make it any easier.'

'Of course it doesn't.'

'I've tried to keep myself busy,' Tony continued. 'First it was doing stuff around the house - Brenda had a long list that she'd been building up for me. So the first couple of months I was busy, and I didn't really notice my career was over. But then the big jobs were done, I was sitting around the house twiddling my thumbs, listening to the clock ticking, and all I could see was this big lot of nothing stretching into the distance, until, you know, death.'

'You're not making retirement sound very appealing,' Cullen joked softly.

'It isn't.'

'But what about all your challenges? The speeches, today?'

Tony shrugged. 'Just trying to fill the void.'

Cullen didn't quite know what to say. In truth, he could imagine what it felt like, to leave the job you loved, to lose your identity, and it didn't feel good at all. 'It will get better,' he tried. 'Book another holiday. You really enjoyed that cruise.'

'A sticking plaster.'

'You'll find a way,' Cullen continued. 'It's early days, and it will take time to get used to things. How about contacting the employee counselling service? They're supposed to be pretty good with things like this.'

'They're the ones who suggested I set myself some challenges,' Tony revealed, taking a big glug of beer.

'Fair enough. Well, it sounds like you're doing the right thing.'

'I hope so. I am jealous of you, Paul,' he said, taking Cullen by surprise.

'Jealous?'

'You've got years left,' he said. 'Fifteen, maybe twenty. When I think of all the adventures, all the excitement you'll have at BTP here in London, I'd give anything to be in your position.'

Now it was Cullen's face that darkened.

It was time to tell Tony the truth.

5

Present Day

'WHAT'S UP, BOSS?' Tony said.

'Nothing,' Cullen replied, rather unconvincingly, surprised but not particularly disappointed that Tony had been so perceptive, and so quickly.

'You look pensive. Like something's weighing heavy on your mind,' his drinking partner added, taking a sip from the pint. He placed it down carefully on the table, all the time keeping his eyes on Cullen, knowing that he was right. 'Either that, or it's indigestion.'

'Am I so obvious?' Cullen asked, flipping and catching a beer mat, before repeating the feat with three stacked together.

Tony smiled winningly. 'You forget, I'm an experienced detective with over thirty years of dedicated service.'

'I am pretty obvious though, aren't I?' Cullen ran a hand

across his face. 'Danny asked me the same question yesterday. I told him I was just tired.'

'And he took that?'

Cullen smiled. 'He had to, I guess.'

Detective Inspector Danny Lomax, his deputy in the British Transport Police's Serious and Organised Crime Unit, had nodded at the time, seemingly satisfied with the explanation, and Cullen had felt no compulsion to reveal what was really going on. At least not yet.

But Tony was different. He had worked closely with him for years, their families were friends. They'd holidayed together. Tony wasn't just a colleague.

He was the one person he would tell.

'So what's wrong?' Tony probed, scenting victory. 'Issue with a case? I know how you sometimes get when things aren't going the right way.'

Cullen shook his head.

Tony suddenly looked more concerned. 'Something with the family? Sarah's okay?'

'Sarah's fine.'

His brow furrowed deeply. 'You're not well?'

'Nothing like that,' Cullen reassured his worried friend. 'I'm fighting fit. At least as far as I know.'

Cullen was conscious not to take his health for granted. The fate of his friend, Philip, struck down in his forties with early onset dementia, had been a devastatingly hard lesson.

Don't take anything for granted.

Tony's heart attack had also reinforced that feeling of vulnerability to life's twists and turns. But in many ways, that hadn't been so much of a surprise - Tony hadn't lived the healthiest of lifestyles. But Philip had been a super-fit, healthy rugby league international, whose life had been robbed from him.

'Spit it out, Paul.'

Cullen nodded, playing the words around in his head. 'I'm leaving.'

Tony Beswick looked genuinely gobsmacked, the pint suspended between the table and his open mouth.

He knew exactly what Cullen meant.

'I've decided to move back up North,' Cullen added. 'I've been thinking about it for a good while now.'

'To be with Sarah,' Tony said at last sombrely.

'To be with Sarah,' Cullen confirmed. 'And Philip.'

Tony nodded. 'I'd be lying to say that I'm not gutted to hear that,' he admitted. 'You'll be a massive loss to the team. You've brought so much. Your leadership, it will be missed. A lot.'

Cullen shrugged away his real feelings. 'Things change. People change. Someone else will come along, pick up the baton and take things forward.'

'I'm not sure who,' Tony said. 'But that shouldn't be your concern.'

'It is though,' Cullen replied. 'I am concerned that the team are looked after, when I go.'

'I know you are,' Tony said. 'Which is what makes you a hard person to replace.'

'You're very kind, Tony.' Cullen smiled. 'But don't make this harder than it already is.'

Tony nodded. 'Have you spoken to Maggie about it?'

Detective Superintendent Maggie Ferguson, Cullen's boss and head of the British Transport Police's Central Division.

'I haven't even told Sarah yet,' Cullen revealed, prompting a surprised reaction from Tony.

'I know, I know,' Cullen acknowledged, his hands aloft. 'But I wanted to get it clear in my own mind first, I wanted to be rock solid in my thinking, before talking to Sarah.'

'You think she'll try and talk you out of it.'

'In short, yes.'

'Don't you want to be talked out of it?'

'I could be talked out of it,' Cullen admitted, dodging the question slightly. 'Unless I'm prepared.'

'Then why are you even considering it? If you don't mind me asking?'

'This is sounding like an interrogation.'

Tony smiled. 'Force of habit.'

'I guess I wanted this,' Cullen admitted, thinking through his response. 'I wanted you to challenge me.'

'Well go on, then. Make your case, Paul.'

Tony sat back and folded his arms, as if he really was on the other side of the desk in an interview room.

'I don't want things to carry on the way they are,' Cullen began. 'Me, living out a suitcase in a London hotel room, with Sarah over a hundred miles away. Seeing each other every other weekend, at most. It's just...not...the way it should be.'

Tony thought on that. 'I understand. Brenda drives me mad sometimes, but if I couldn't see her, it would be awful.'

'It's been over six months since Sarah moved back up.'

'That's a long time to be apart.'

'It feels longer,' Cullen admitted.

Tony sat back. 'Life is short,' he said. 'You need to do what your instincts tell you. Things will work out - career-wise, you'll thrive wherever you are, Paul. But the most important thing is your family.'

6

Previously

PROFESSOR BEN BRODY eyed the audience through his round, wire-rimmed glasses, clasped his hands together and smiled a winning smile.

'People of the good town of Hope,' he began, the smile fading. 'First of all I want to thank you, and particularly the good Mayor here, for inviting me to help in this troublesome situation. I know there's a lot of anxiety relating to what happened three week's ago and I promise you that, for as long as it takes, for as long as you want me to be involved, I will be here for you all.'

He paused and looked across at Curtis, giving a single nod as affirmation of his promise.

'But,' he said, returning his attention to the audience. 'I'm afraid that some of the things I'm about to say, will be difficult to hear. I'm sorry, but I'm not here to give you the same comforting message that our good friend Dr. Peters from the

Environmental Protection Agency has just given. As I said, I'm aware of the anxieties across your community, within each of your homes, so if anyone here doesn't feel up to hearing what I have to say, then please, by all means, feel free to leave now and we can update you later. I promise I won't be offended!'

The Professor looked around but no-one moved.

'In that case, I'll begin,' he said, clicking through to the first slide of his presentation.

'As you all know, three weeks' ago, at a quarter past midnight, a freight train owned by Deep Distribution and carrying a range of toxic substances derailed outside the town, with thirty of its one hundred and twenty cars leaving the track. As I'm sure you are all aware, The National Transportation Safety Board, which investigates all major rail accidents in the United States, has concluded that the derailment was caused by a malfunction of an axle - the rod connecting the train wheels. It's important to note that the investigation into the derailment is still ongoing, with a final report due sometime in the next few weeks, but the evidence of it being the axle is strong and up to now, uncontested. Unfortunately, the locomotive was not fitted with the gold standard, internationally recommended electronic braking system. If it had been, then the emergency brakes would have been engaged simultaneously across all one hundred and twenty train cars, greatly limiting the extent of the derailment and very likely avoiding the awful consequences of the chemical fire and explosions. But as it didn't have this system, and used only conventional, old-style brakes, the braking happened front to back, causing a ripple effect that magnified the problem along the length of the locomotive.'

Professor Brody gazed around at the captivated audience. 'Any questions so far?'

One hand went up.

'The lady in the far corner.'

The middle aged lady waited for the roving microphone to reach her. 'Do the companies not have to have these better braking systems? I mean, why wouldn't they?'

'Cost,' the Professor replied. 'This was an older set, and could have been retrofitted to meet the higher standards, but it often comes down to money. There was a law brought in following a derailment in 2012, that required all trains carrying toxic substances to be fitted with the electronic braking system. But it was lobbied against by the freight industry, including Deep Distribution, and I'm afraid it was rescinded by the previous White House administration.'

The lady nodded and passed the microphone back, her face serious.

The Professor continued. 'The shocking truth is that over twenty million Americans live in areas that are vulnerable to derailment of trains carrying toxic substances. You are in those twenty million. Each year, hundreds of trains pass no more than a few hundred metres of your homes, carrying some of the most dangerous materials on Earth, right past your bedroom window. There are few safeguards.'

'Can you tell us more about the chemicals?' a man shouted out.

'Just about to,' Brody replied. 'As Dr Peters outlined, a number of the train cars were carrying hazardous materials. The most concerning of these is vinyl chloride, which is used in plastic products. Colourless and highly flammable, it was the chief reason for the explosions, and the cars carrying it were located right outside the town. Short term exposure effects include dizziness and drowsiness, which I know a significant number of you reported to the authorities. There were three other chemicals on board, all of which were released into the air following the derailment, explosions and fire; Ethylhexyl acrylate, isobutylene, and ethylene glycol monobutyl. All of these chemicals cause a range of short-term health impacts - shortness of breath, burning of eyes and skin, headaches, nausea. A gas cloud of this nasty group of chemicals was hanging over your town for several hours, so it's little wonder there have been health issues reported among you. Your good Mayor here can testify to the effects,' he added, glancing at Curtis, who coughed on cue.

'You're damn right,' Curtis added, along with many nods from the audience.

The Professor acknowledged the reaction of the room. 'A very important thing,' he said. 'Keep detailed notes about any symptoms. The characteristics of those symptoms, the timings of when they came on, the severity, how it makes you feel. And think medium and longer term. I'm afraid vinyl chloride has been linked with a number of forms of cancer. I don't want to worry you, but you need to be aware and record, record, record. You diarise the hell out of it. Because that is your evidence, your truth, and your power against the big boys who will try and argue that your ill-health has nothing whatsoever to do with what happened here in Hope on that fateful night. And believe me, they will throw the kitchen sink at any case that you try to bring. They are relentless.'

Curtis looked around at his fellow residents. The atmosphere was so tense and Curtis sensed that the message the Professor had just given had increased anxiety levels.

'But!' the Professor said, holding up a finger. 'Do not be afraid of these people. That's what they want - to scare you away. Soon they might write letters to you - they've done it before - it's part of their playbook, to use mind games to dissuade action that might bring them to account. You get contacted by Deep Distribution, or any of their friends, you report it to Curtis here. They will try to drive a wedge between this community, you can mark my words.'

Professor Brody paused. 'I'm sorry that this is a worrying message. On a more positive note, we know that our good friends at the EPA have deemed that air and water samples are now safe for you guys, which is why you have been allowed back. That's obviously a good thing. And I'm pleased to hear that the home screening did not detect any traces of the chemicals in your homes.'

'I don't believe it,' a gruff voiced man shouted. Curtis knew him well. It was Liam Johnson, an old classmate of his, and owner of the town's main convenience store. The microphone was hurriedly passed to him, but he ignored it and projected easily without any amplification. 'They don't know it's safe. What about the dead fish in the creak? And Mrs Stone's chickens, all dead within a week, all of them. They were inside when the accident happened, just like all of us. Then there's the drinking water, to me, it tastes real odd. I've been drinking that water for fifty years, and I know something ain't right. I've been boiling it.'

'And the smell!' another person shouted. 'I swear, the smell is still there.'

There were murmurs of agreement.

'How do we know it ain't making us sick?'

'Which is why it's so important to keep your own records,' Brody replied. 'I'm sure the authorities are doing everything right.' He looked pointedly at Dr. Peters, who was sitting in the front row. 'But there's only so much they can do, so much they can look for and test. You,' he said, pointing at the audience, 'you guys can provide the best evidence of any impacts. I really can't stress that enough.'

'So we just wait to get sicker and sicker,' Liam concluded.

The Professor seemed uncharacteristically lost for words, but he was just mulling over a response to probably the most challenging point of the night so far. 'In terms of acute impacts, I'm afraid what's done is done,' he said at last. 'As for medium and longer term effects of that acute incident, we all need to watch and wait. But on the possible continuing danger posed by what happened, the news based on the evidence we have seems more positive. However, there are proactive things I would like to propose. Top of that list is that I would like the company responsible, Deep Distribution, to help to ensure that this town is safe - they could pay for enhanced environmental sampling, decontamination and remediation of the land. I also propose that the company pays for a longer term study of you guys, so that we can spot any possible health impacts.'

Ben looked across at Curtis. 'Shall I mention the other thing, or would you like to do that yourself?'

Curtis was already shifting in his seat, as if he was going to move himself up on the stage. Tom Bradshaw, a young member of the community jumped up and wheeled Curtis up towards the front. As he was moved, Curtis grabbed the roving microphone.

'Thank you, Tom,' he nodded to his helper, as a cue to the young man that he was okay to sit back down. Curtis turned and addressed the crowd, suppressing another painful shockwave down his back. 'I wanted to thank you all for coming this evening,' he said, trying to make eye contact with each and everyone one of the residents who had turned up for this powerful community show of strength. 'And I promise I won't keep you here much longer. Despite the antics of Deep Distribution, we still have homes to go to. I just wanted to say a couple of final things. Firstly, as you will have heard, we have already begun the process of putting together a legal case to sue Deep Distribution, which will, we hope, cover medical screening for all residents within a thirty mile radius of the derailment. We are arguing - and as you heard from the Professor here - we have a good case, that the company failed to exercise reasonable care to protect local residents from exposure to toxic materials. It is my hope, that the company will do the right thing before this progresses to court. It is a real shame that they did not accept our invitation to attend this evening's meeting, and engage with us. But there is still time for them to begin to try and make things right.'

Curtis craned his neck towards the back of the room.

'And I hope that you guys and girls from the free press, who have been kind enough to attend tonight, can play your part, and spread the word to the rest of America about what has happened to our lovely town and its people. I believe that you can help to bring the company to the table, so please, do your best to get the word out and...'

Curtis's rallying cry was curtailed by a coughing fit. These had been an hourly occurrence ever since that night; a result of damage to his lungs, with inflammation irritating him. The doctors hadn't been able to say whether the damage would heal, but he really hoped so.

Thankfully this particular bout was soothed by some sips from the glass of water that Ben Brody passed over to him.

'Thank you, Ben,' he said. 'So, I think I'd better stop now,' he said, worried that the coughing might start up again. Thank you again. Together we can win this fight!'

The room broke out into applause, which to Curtis's amazement quickly became a standing ovation. He blushed at the reaction; even the guy from the EPA was on his feet, clapping. This had gone better than he even could have hoped.

But in that moment of elation, the darker thoughts returned to him.

Would they be clapping him if they knew the truth?

His smile faded as the question ate away at his insides. Hope was an amazing place with amazing people - there was no place on earth where he would rather be.

But like all small, otherwise quiet backwater towns, it could be a hotbed of gossip, where someone's business could quickly become everyone's business. And the people of Hope had long memories, particularly when it came to transgressions.

Even more with a fallen hero.

It had happened before, a number of times. There was Jasper Conway, the former police chief, who it turned out had been stealing alcohol from the Johnson's convenience store. He'd been tracked by a couple of nosey local residents, who had not only seen him taking the liquor, but had also watched him consume the bottle of whisky behind the town hall and dispose of it in the public bin.

The popular Jasper - a pillar of the community - had been left shamed and vilified. He'd lived in Hope all his life, but had moved to the city shortly after the news of his thieving and alcohol problems had broke.

As far as Curtis knew, Jasper had never been back to the town since.

The applause finally began to peter out as Curtis made another promise to himself that he was going to try and make things right. The internal struggle would be more difficult than even the fight against Daniel Deep, and there was, to him, even more to lose.

But it was a fight he needed to win.

The smile returned as he felt that renewed sense of positivity. He would use this energy from the community, and win against the odds on both fronts.

Losing was not an option.

7

Present Day

'COME IN.'

Paul Cullen stepped into Maggie Ferguson's office, having received the call to come upstairs just five minutes earlier. He'd been talking to Danny about the ongoing case of a series of increasingly violent robberies that had taken place across the rail network in the South East.

Maggie wanted an urgent update.

'Morning, Ma'am,' Cullen replied, as he took the seat in response to Maggie's gesture.

'Morning,' she said flatly, hammering out words at the keyboard like she was trying to break it, her attention somewhere else. 'I'm still bothered by the ongoing case,' she said, continuing to type. 'It's like a festering wound, and a wound left to fester only gets worse.'

Cullen nodded. To Cullen's intense frustration, they'd yet to identify the masked perpetrator, despite extensive CCTV footage and a mass distribution leaflet campaign targeting commuters. 'I feel the same way.'

The individual had started small, snatching bags that had been left unattended on station platforms, targeting the smaller countryside and suburban stations that didn't have barrier access - enabling them to escape with ease and at speed.

That was last year.

Now they'd become emboldened by their success, seeking out victims and ripping items from their possession - mobile phones and bags mainly. Often the speed at which this had been done meant that the targets hadn't even realised what was happening before the thief was off and away.

'The event of two weeks' ago, it worries me,' she said. 'The way the press have picked up on it, what are they calling him?'

'The Masked Mugger.'

'Yes, the Masked Mugger,' she mused. 'I don't like the way things are going, one little bit.'

The case had changed dramatically two weeks ago.

The thief had struck again. This time they had targeted someone who had fought back, a gym-fit man in his thirties who did not want to relinquish his top of the range iPhone to the assailant. In the ensuing struggle, all captured on the station's CCTV, the thief had stabbed the man in the stomach before making their escape.

Thankfully a fellow passenger had arrived at the quiet country station shortly after the attack, and within a few minutes the air ambulance arrived.

Without such rapid treatment, the medics had been clear that this could have been a murder enquiry.

It had sharpened everyone's minds at British Transport Police HQ.

'Can you remind me what we're doing to step up the hunt for this person?' Maggie asked, by way of a challenge.

Cullen was ready and didn't miss a beat.

'We've allocated more uniformed officers across the south east network, to patrol during off-peak hours especially, but also peak too. From next week there will be significantly increased visibility, which I hope will act as a clear deterrent.'

Maggie didn't look overly impressed, and Cullen knew her well enough to know what she was thinking.

'But this person has to be caught,' Cullen continued, not leaving the gap for his boss to interject. 'So we're deploying a number of plain clothes officers, who will be the eyes and ears across the network.'

Maggie Ferguson nodded. 'Good. That's good. How many?'

'Fifty, maybe just over initially, on rotation.'

'Can we increase that number if we need to?'

'Unlikely, from our core workforce. But I've been talking to colleagues in the local forces, and they might be able to provide plain clothes alongside the additional uniformed patrols they've already promised.'

'Keep the possibility open,' she said. 'Let's see what we can do on our own first, but hold that in reserve.'

'Certainly.'

'Paul. We need to get this person before he does any more harm.'

'We will.'

'Glad to hear it.'

Cullen could see that she had already moved on in her mind to something else. This is how their meetings always worked - Cullen readied for the next item on the agenda as Maggie sifted through the list in her head. Often it felt like an interrogation, and Cullen had wondered more than once what Maggie Ferguson had been like as a more junior officer, facing off against suspects on the other side of the table.

He didn't doubt she had been a fearsome adversary.

'Have you heard of Daniel Deep?' Maggie asked, sitting back in her chair.

Cullen thought on it. 'The name rings a bell.'

Maggie smiled. 'He knows you.'

Cullen searched his memories some more. The unusual name definitely did seem familiar, but still he couldn't pin anything down as to where he had heard it before. Usually he was good with names, particularly when he needed to be, but in this case he couldn't reach the answer. 'Any clues?' he ventured to joke.

'One of the richest men in the world,' she said. 'Silicon Valley entrepreneur. Founded Deep Insight technology company, specialising in socio-demographic data usage. Began as a start-up but is now worth more than the GDP of most countries. He worked for the Republicans during the last Presidential Election, targeting potential voters through key demographics and behavioural insights. Also did some work for the Conservatives recently, with deep insight analytics.'

'I'm not really into technology,' Cullen explained, wondering what all this was about. Maggie might as well have been talking Dutch with all that jargon. 'So he's like Bill Gates?'

'Sort of,' Maggie said kindly. 'But more data analytics driven. One of the most powerful people in the world. Already a billionaire.'

'I dislike him already,' Cullen quipped. He was still processing what Maggie had said. 'You said he knows me?'

'Yes.'

Cullen waited for an explanation, but realised as Maggie suppressed a smile that she was being uncharacteristically playful and was enjoying leaving him dangling for a bit.

So he played along. 'He's a fan of mine. He's in the Paul Cullen fan club,' he dead-panned.

Maggie clicked her fingers into a point. 'Correct first time.'

Cullen was even more confused. 'Okay, fill me in on how a Silicon Valley billionaire knows anything about a detective in the British Transport Police.'

'Daniel Deep spends quite a bit of time in the UK,' she explained. 'He is very proud of his Scottish ancestry - one of his distant relatives emigrated to the States from Scotland - so Deep bought a castle in the Scottish Highlands.'

'Naturally.'

'And he travels down to London a lot for business - his company have their European HQ here - so he's very aware of what goes on in the UK, including our organisation. He's very proud of his Scottish ancestry and makes it his business to know what's happening.'

'Most people who were born here don't know there is a British Transport Police,' Cullen quipped, 'and that included my parents, let alone an American whose great-great-great grandfather once wore a kilt.'

It was true. When he had told his now-passed mother and father that he wanted to pursue a career in the British Transport Police, they had looked at him with blank expressions.

Many people had seen the transport police on their journeys across the rail network, but often saw just the uniform and not the distinction between them and the regular police force.

'Daniel Deep is a huge railway enthusiast,' Maggie explained. 'As well as his insight company, he owns the biggest rail freight operation in the USA, Deep Distribution, and has been lifelong train buff - he's President of the American Model Railroad Association and has the largest model railway track in the world in his Californian residence. He always travels by train between Scotland and London, and is a big advocate for rail over short haul air travel - including lobbying the government to follow the French and take action.'

Cullen took it all in. 'You know a lot about him.'

'Wikipedia,' she replied. 'There's a lot of information about him on the internet. A lot.'

'So he's into trains,' Cullen continued. 'But where do I come in, and what's this all about?'

'We were contacted by Mr Deep via the Mayor's Office,' she said. 'He's a good friend of the Mayor - they became friends a few years ago, about the time he set up his London HQ.'

That figured.

'I then spoke to his representative a few days ago,' she continued. 'He's about to launch a new rail service in the UK - a luxury sleeper service - running from London up to the Scottish Highlands. The plan is to expand it across Europe, connecting the major cities. But the London-Scotland route will be first.'

'I still don't understand where I fit in to all this.'

'The inaugural trip will take place this weekend. It will be a test run, with guests invited by Daniel Deep. They will travel on the sleeper from King's Cross, overnight to the Scottish Highlands, and stay one night at his residence by Loch Laggan, before returning the next evening on the sleeper.'

'Sounds lovely.'

'I'm glad you think so,' she said cryptically. 'The trip will be high profile, with lots of media interest, and the guests will be equally high profile - including figures from the world of business and politics. Mr Deep wants to ensure that everything runs smoothly on the journey.'

'I imagine he does.'

'He wants us - the British Transport Police - to ensure the safety and security of the guests.'

'But our remit..'

'Ordinarily our remit would not extend to this, I agree,' Maggie cut in, correctly reading where Paul was going to go with it, 'but this is a special circumstance and one which I am sympathetic to. As I said, Daniel Deep is close to the Mayor, and his investment in the UK and London is significant and worthy of recognising, where we are able to accommodate.'

Cullen got the politics here. But that didn't mean that he liked it, or had to roll over like some kind of lapdog just because the guy was best buddies with the Mayor. 'I don't think it's a good idea.'

'I thought you might say that,' Maggie replied. 'And I do understand your position, Paul, of course I do.'

'But...'

'But, as I said, this is a special situation, and I wouldn't have even considered it if I didn't think that it was appropriate and useful for the force.'

Paul waited for the pregnant pause.

'I guess we could send one of our officers,' he conceded.

'I'm sure someone would enjoy the luxury weekend break. It isn't much notice, though. We might struggle to get someone of appropriate seniority.'

He didn't like the way Maggie was looking at him.

'He wants you to accompany him,' she replied.

Cullen blinked. 'Just me?'

'Just you. He was quite clear on that.'

'What? Me or nothing? Go back to him, tell him that we will provide him with one of our people, maybe two if they have the room.'

'I did suggest just that,' she revealed, 'but the offer was refused. He wants you.'

Cullen shook his head, frustrated about police affairs being dictated to by this person. 'But...why?'

She shrugged. 'As I said, he's a fan. Asked for you by name. He certainly knew who you were.'

Another shake of the head. 'I didn't go into this to play personal bodyguard for some billionaire.'

'Of course you didn't,' Maggie agreed. 'But you did take this role with the full knowledge that sometimes you will be expected to do things that you don't want to do, for the sake of the wider organisation and system.'

Cullen tried a different tact. 'One officer, me, whoever, it's not going to exactly guarantee security, not one hundred percent.'

'I wouldn't underestimate your abilities, Paul,' Maggie smiled. 'But joking aside, I see this more of a symbolic role. He wants you on board, not to be his bodyguard - he's probably got a few of them already lined up - but to be part of the ride.'

'Me and the hand-picked VIPs?'

'You and the hand-picked VIPs.'

'Do I have a choice?' Cullen challenged.

'Of course,' she replied, surprising him a little. 'We always have a choice. But all decisions come with consequences.'

'Indeed.'

'Look, Paul, have a think about this,' Maggie said, softening. 'Take your time...'

Cullen laughed. 'The train's about to leave.'

'Consider it today,' Maggie continued, 'then get back to me with your decision. If you really feel so strongly about it, then of course, I'll be disappointed, and so will the Mayor. But I'll understand.'

She didn't really look like she would understand, but even to pretend was a surprise to Paul.

'It's not our normal operational business,' she admitted. 'But strategically, one could argue that it is very core to what we are supposed to do. And look on the bright side, Paul, it's a free holiday.'

'I'll give it some careful thought,' he conceded. 'But the answer is probably no.'

'Just think about it, Paul,' Maggie replied, not showing any outward sign of the disappointment that she must surely have been feeling. 'I appreciate this has just been landed on you, and you need time to think things through.'

'I'll think about it,' Cullen promised.

'Really, Paul, what could possibly go wrong?'

'Murder on the Orient Express,' Cullen muttered, as he left the room with his potential new assignment playing on his mind.

8

Previously

CURTIS WAITED for the milk to heat up on the hob, ready to add to the hot chocolate mixture. Cindy had already retired to bed and would be asleep by now, but it would be another hour until Curtis would try.

He smiled to himself as he poured the milk onto the chocolate powder, thinking about how well things had gone at the community meeting.

It really couldn't have turned out any better.

And tonight - if only for tonight - he would try and forget about those other bad things strangling his well-being, and focus on the positives.

Tomorrow he would catch up with Professor Brody, who was staying overnight in town at Mrs Turner's guest house. Curtis and the Professor had set a breakfast date at the diner in town, where they would plot their next move.

Curtis had just settled into his armchair, remote control in hand, when there as a sharp knock at the door.

He looked across at the clock on the fireplace, his pulse quickening at the unexpected, sudden interruption. It was a quarter past eleven.

Who would call at such an anti-social hour?

He froze in the chair, spooked. Occasionally because of his Mayoral role he would receive late-night visitors, but it was pretty rare and hadn't happened for a good year or so. Mostly people knew to respect boundaries, both regarding time and place to engage him in his official role.

Another knock - faster and harder.

Maybe it was an emergency.

Between rising from the chair and reaching the door, another thought occurred to him - it could be Professor Brody. Maybe something was up at the guest house, or he was calling around to borrow a toothbrush. The phone signal around Hope was notoriously bad, so it was plausible that the Professor would have been forced to hotfoot it the short distance to Curtis's should anything be needed.

He opened the door in a much more relaxed manner, with the thought of the amiable Professor standing on the other side.

But it wasn't him.

It was a dark-suited, middle-aged man, who was holding something by his side.

Taken by surprise, Curtis made to close the door ever so slightly - without it looking too impolite, but the man pushed past him and strode into the living room.

'Can I help you?' Curtis asked, hurrying after him, his words betraying his fear. 'You can't just...'

'Mr Chesterfield,' the stranger said, spinning a large envelope onto the coffee table, where it narrowly missed the untouched hot chocolate. 'I've come bearing a gift.'

Curtis looked at the envelope, utterly confused, and then back at the unwelcome guest. Face to face under the light of the living room, the visitor was familiar, and Curtis finally placed him. 'You were at the community meeting,' he said, 'sitting at the back with the media?'

The man smiled. 'I'm here to make you an offer,' he stated, ignoring Curtis's question. 'Inside that envelope is ten thousand dollars in cash. It's all yours, if you drop the case.'

'You're from Deep Distribution?' Curtis said, still jittery at the man's brazen invasion of his property.

'An associate,' the man replied, taking a look around the room as if he was sizing it up for a potential house purchase. 'As I said, you take the money, drop the case, and everyone's a winner.'

'Apart from the people of Hope,' Curtis replied in as strong a voice as he could muster. He looked at the bulging package, feeling both tempted and repulsed by the offer. 'Please, take your money and tell Mr Deep that I can't be bought.' He picked up the weighty envelope, thoughts of all those bank notes in his head, and held it out towards the man.

The man made no move to take it. 'You need this money, Curtis,' he said, squaring up to him.

'I don't,' he replied, already with a sinking feeling, wondering whether what the man had just said was an unfortunate co-incidence.

'Don't you?'

Curtis maintained his resolve. 'I can't take this money.'

The man's expression darkened. 'I think you can, and you will,' he said, fishing a folded piece of paper from his inside jacket pocket. He handed it to Curtis. 'We know all about your not-so-little gambling problem, Mr Mayor. But the question is, does Cindy?'

Curtis read the piece of paper with horror. They knew. It was all there, somehow; his online gaming accounts, revealing the terrifying depths of his debt. He gripped the paper so hard that it scrunched at the edges. 'Where did you get this?'

'You think anything you do online is private?' the man laughed. 'It really isn't that difficult. And that's the sad fact; people in corporations know more about you, your secrets, your desires, your vices, than those who you share a bed with.'

Curtis felt like he could be vomit.

He looked up at the man, shaking. 'You can't tell Cindy. It would break her.'

'It would break your marriage, don't you mean?' the man replied cooly, sensing the balance of power was tipping decidedly in his favour. 'Break your reputation too, Mr Mayor, among the community.'

Curtis shook his head, looking again at the devastating debt laid bare before him. The man was right - if news got out about his gambling problem, it would be the end of him in this town. He looked down again at the envelope, wondering if he could take the money and somehow still do the right thing.

Or would it just make things worse?

The man saw the hesitation on Curtis's face and leaned in close. 'You need to make a decision now,' he said, his voice low and threatening. 'I walk out the door with that money, and the deal is off. And this,' he said, snatching the piece of paper back off Curtis, 'will go up on the town noticeboard -

along with some other interesting facts about Mayor Curtis Chesterfield. I may even put a call in to the lovely Cindy, just to make sure she gets the message.'

Curtis was torn. 'It's not just me,' he said. 'This isn't just about me. It's the people of the town; they want justice. Even if I stopped what I was doing, dropped the case, it wouldn't make a difference.'

'It will,' the man said simply. 'The town look to you for leadership, for direction. I saw tonight how they follow you. You tell them that it isn't in their best interests to pursue a legal route. Explain that you've spoken to the company and have agreed on a way forward. Mr Deep wants to help you, he will put in place some health monitoring, do some clean up. The town gets looked after, you get bailed out of your predicament.'

Curtis looked again at the package, running a hand through his hair.

'Make the sensible decision, Curtis,' the man pressed.

'Curtis? Is everything okay? I thought I could hear voices?'

Curtis looked up in horror as Cindy appeared at the bottom of the stairs, her face worried and arms wrapped around her dressing gown. She looked in confusion at the strange man in her house.

'It's okay,' Curtis said, trying desperately to think on his feet, as the man smiled a hello. 'This man is from the freight company, Deep Distribution. He came here to offer the town a deal.'

Cindy tried to take in the news, still obviously puzzled by the timing.

'It's okay, you go back to bed, love,' Curtis added.

Cindy nodded and retreated back upstairs.

'So we have a deal?' the man smiled.

Curtis nodded, unable to put his decision to words.

'Then I'll leave you be,' the man said, clasping his hands together. 'Have a good night, Curtis. I'd put that somewhere safe for now,' he added, gesturing at the envelope of cash. And do try and stay off those gambling sites from now on; they're a path to disaster.'

Curtis, willing the man to leave and never return, shepherded him to the door, closing it behind him without another word.

Curtis leant against the back of the door, pressing his weight into the wood, feeling shaken and alone.

He might have saved himself by grabbing at this grubby, desperate deal.

But what had he lost?

9

Present Day

CULLEN RETURNED BACK DOWNSTAIRS to the main office, nodding a hello at colleagues as they looked up from their computer screens. A couple who he spotted on their mobile phones placed them screen down on their desks when they realised he was present.

He made his way over to where his deputy DI Danny Lomax was on the phone, in what sounded like a frustrating conversation. Danny pulled a face at Cullen.

'Look, I've got to go now,' Danny said into the receiver. 'But please do give it some serious thought. This is a real priority not just for us, but everyone across the region. It could easily spill out to other community settings - and may already have done. Plus these are members of your community who are being put at risk...sure...will do. Speak soon.'

'Trouble?' Cullen asked, as Danny slammed down the desk phone so hard that he was at risk of breaking it.

'Sorry, Boss,' Danny said, dragging a hand across his face as he lent back in the chair. 'You know, sometimes I wonder if we're actually all on the same side. I mean, aren't we all trying to do the same thing - keep the public safe?'

'Let's chat,' Cullen said, gesturing towards his office.

Danny followed, closing the door behind him as they entered the room.

'Who was it?' Cullen asked. 'Hampshire?'

Paul had asked Danny to ring around the police forces across the South East of England, to garner support for stepping up work to catch the Masked Mugger. What Cullen had told Maggie Ferguson had been only a half-truth - there had been support by forces to provide additional manpower in the form of limited uniformed patrols, but it was tokenistic and hardly likely to make much of an impact. Plus although there had been a promise, it wasn't yet confirmed.

On the subject of provision of plain clothes officers to supplement the Transport Police, there was more push-back. Capacity was limited, he got that.

'Hampshire, yes,' Danny confirmed, still looking exasperated. 'How did you guess?'

Hampshire had been particularly negative in their response, even though it was the location of the latest, most serious incident and had also seen the highest number of incidents overall.

'Who did you speak to? Patterson?'

The Chief Constable, Peter Patterson, was a particular character, who guarded his independence and had always seemed to only barely tolerate cooperation with the BTP. Cullen had heard via several sources that he and Maggie Ferguson had clashed at a national police chiefs' meeting a couple of years ago, which probably explained the attitude.

'His underling. Carling,' Danny confirmed. 'Was less than helpful, to put it politely.'

'And put honestly?' Cullen said. Danny was a valued and trusted close senior colleague, plainly spoken, which was often just what was needed to cut through the crap.

Danny smiled mischievously at being given the license to speak freely. 'A bit of an unhelpful bastard.'

'Carling is Patterson's mouth piece; nothing more. We won't get a proactive response from him,' Cullen stated. Cullen had met Dominic Carling a few times, and hadn't been impressed. It was clear how he'd progressed within the force, and it wasn't a particular talent at policing or a personable, helpful demeanour. Unlike Carling, at least the top man Patterson did seem like a decent guy on a one-to-one basis, despite his apparent organisational grudge. 'Did you ask to speak with the Chief Constable?'

'Yes.'

Cullen thought as much. 'Let me give Peter a call. If I can get past his PA.'

'Good luck, Boss,' Danny smiled.

'We've got to get this cracked,' Cullen said. 'And we can't do it without the help of the local forces. They'll soon come running if there's a death.'

'Indeed.'

'Maggie wants it to be the highest priority. As you might imagine.'

'You just met with her?'

'Yes. I'm afraid I might have overpromised. But we just need to make sure that we don't underdeliver.'

'Agreed.'

Cullen thought on the rest of the earlier conversation.

'Take a seat,' he said to Danny, who was still standing near the door.

Danny pulled up a seat.

'What do you know about Daniel Deep?' Cullen asked, betting that Danny would be much more up to speed on world personalities than he was. He knew from the years working with him, that Danny was a keen follower of celebrity culture, in a way that Cullen wasn't.

'One of the richest men in the world,' Danny said, not disappointing his friend and boss. 'A billionaire. And a bit of an idiot.'

Cullen's interest was certainly piqued. 'Idiot? Why do you say that?'

'From what I've heard on the news,' he replied. 'He has a reputation for taking over companies - rivals - and crushing them.'

'Really?'

'About six months ago there was a story about how he took over a British data analytics company, promised that he'd honour their independence. But he then asked everyone to sign up to some crazy workload demands, or face the sack. Basically the demands were designed to drive people out, something like wanting the UK staff to work on California time. It worked, of course. The staff left and the company collapsed. He just wanted to absorb the competition, drain their resources, and throw out the rest.'

'The people.'

'The people. Yes. He's done it many times before. It's the way he works, and prospers.'

'So he's ruthless,' Cullen noted.

'Ruthless and also very strange.'

'Strange? How so?'

'You really don't know anything about him, do you?' Danny smiled. 'Daniel Deep is obsessed with his health. And I mean obsessed. I read an article about him last year - the guy thinks he can reverse the ageing process.'

'Reverse the ageing process?'

'Yes, through a combination of intense physical exercise, some very strange diet, vitamin and mineral supplements and injections, and not a small amount of surgery.'

'So he's not a subscriber to growing old gracefully.'

'Definitely not.'

As they spoke, Cullen did a quick image search on his computer for the man. Most of the images that appeared either showed him speaking at events, commanding the stage with a wrap around microphone, or dressed in fitness gear pounding sun-drenched, San Francisco sidewalks.

'How old is he?' Cullen asked, studying Deep's face in one of the close up pictures.

'Early fifties,' Danny replied.

'I guess he does look good for his age,' Cullen noted. 'But I'd still put him late forties.'

Danny laughed. 'He wouldn't want to hear that.'

'No, I imagine not,' Cullen said, clicking off the search page. He'd seen enough. 'How do you know so much about him?'

Danny looked surprised. 'He's quite high profile,' he replied. 'Very vocal on social media.'

'That would explain why I don't really know who he is.'

Cullen hated social media, and didn't engage with any of the platforms. Why would he want to subject himself to the rantings and ramblings of strangers?

'Fair point,' Danny conceded. 'Although he's on the mainstream news from time to time. Particularly with his actions recently. Why the interest?'

'Because he seems to know me.'

Danny actually laughed at the incredulity of it. 'He knows who you are? Sorry, Boss, didn't mean to laugh, but...'

Cullen held up his hands. 'Now, Danny, I know it's hard to believe that my fame has traveled, but there you go.'

'Seriously though,' Danny said. 'How does Daniel Deep know who you are? And what's it all about?'

Cullen explained about the sleeper train and how the billionaire had asked for him personally via the Mayor's Office to join the maiden voyage this coming weekend, to provide security.

'Sounds odd,' Danny noted. 'No offence, but it just seems weird. Doesn't it?'

'It seems weird,' Cullen agreed.

'Are you going to do it?'

'Let's just say that I wasn't very enthusiastic about the idea of coming running just because some millionaire...billionaire from America wants a British Transport Police officer on board his new train. I told Maggie I'd think about it, but the answer would probably be no.'

'That's what I thought you'd say,' Danny smiled. 'And how did the chief take it?'

'Poker faced. She put on a bit of soft pressure, talked about how it was important for the force to be amenable to requests from the Mayor's associates. She thinks I'll change my mind once I have time to think things over.'

'And will you?'

'Before this conversation with you, probably not,' Cullen admitted. 'Actually I was pretty determined to stick to my guns, especially with how busy we are at the moment and the focus on the thefts. But now...'

'Don't tell me I've persuaded you,' he scoffed in genuine disbelief. 'If anything, I thought I might have put you off. Did I not paint enough of a picture of what an idiot and possible psychopath Daniel Deep is?'

'Actually, you did. Certainly enough to pique my interest.' Cullen played with the pen on his desk, tapping it against the wood. 'What would you say? Would you do it?'

'Free holiday on a luxury train,' Danny shrugged. 'A stay in a Scottish castle. What's not to like? And as you say, intriguing. Why would Daniel Deep request you? I mean, no offence.'

'He wants the best of the best,' Cullen joked. 'He could have chosen anyone, but he picked me. Weird. I want to find out why. And the only way of doing that, is accepting his offer.'

'I agree,' Danny said. 'But having said all that, I would have thought you'd want to steer clear of billionaires from now on.'

Danny was referring to what had happened with Sir Kenneth New, the billionaire who had been involved in the case of Natalie Long. Natalie, a close university friend of Cullen's daughter, Amy, had disappeared after attending a recruitment weekend at one of New's luxury properties in Mayfair. The ensuing investigation had pitted Cullen against Sir Kenneth, who hadn't exactly been an innocent party in the events.

'And you'd be right,' Cullen said.

Kenneth New was an odious character, with a history of sexually assaulting female work colleagues, and had certainly put Cullen off the super-rich for life with both his behaviour and entitled attitude. And yet, Cullen had revelled in sparring with the man, and ultimately coming out victorious. As much as Cullen would hate to admit it, maybe the detective from an unashamedly working class background was a willing fighter in some deep-seated social class war against those who thought they were above others.

'So why accept the offer?' Danny pressed.

Cullen had made up his mind. 'Daniel Deep asking for me to go on that trip is a mystery, and you know how I just can't resist a good mystery.'

10

Present Day

CULLEN SAT AT THE DESK, head resting against his hands, as he stared at the wall. He looked out through the window at his colleagues working hard in the open plan area, imagining his final day, when he would walk out on them, most likely forever.

He could wait a few more days...weeks. But for what? To prolong making the decision that he knew deep down that he had to make. And yet still, he longed to resist - to hang on to what he had, what he loved, for as long as possible. He knew that as soon as the announcement was made, as soon as the team knew he was leaving, everything would change.

The team would immediately begin to move on, and so would he.

He pondered things some more. There would be a three month notice period, and he needed to start that clock ticking as soon as possible.

Delaying the news wasn't a good idea.

He picked up the desk phone and punched in the number. There was no time like the present.

'Maggie, it's Paul...'

'Yes. I have thought some more about the sleeper train assignment...and yes, I am happy to oblige...yes...I understand it's important...there was something else that I wanted to talk to you about...it's best done face to face...okay, great, thanks, I'll be right up.'

Cullen's heart was pounding as he placed the receiver back down on the holder. He didn't feel ready for this - for the finality of it all.

What the hell was he doing?

He didn't even have another job lined up. He would have three months to find something that would work with being back up in the North West of England. Yes, he'd had some tentative, preliminary discussions with people up there, and there was the possibility of a new senior role working out of Manchester, but the post hadn't even been agreed yet at Board level, never mind advertised. And if it did get that far, there was no guarantee that he would get it.

He exited the office, deep in thought, and nearly ran straight into Danny, who pulled up sharply.

'Whoa, Boss, nearly had a coming together there!' he said, surprised. 'Hey, are you okay? You look...'

'I'm fine,' Cullen dismissed, stepping past him and heading for the stairs.

He moved into the stairwell, greeting another couple of colleagues he passed as they were on their way down. He took the few flights more slowly, giving himself some more thinking time.

Had he set off something prematurely? Should he have spoken to Sarah first about this momentous decision? After all, it involved her deeply and there would be financial implications. She might also blame herself, if she felt he had given up his career because of her and Philip.

At least if they had talked it through beforehand, there would have been the opportunity to convince her that he had thought carefully about things, and had made the decision for the very best of reasons.

Cullen reached the top of the stairs, his mind now more knotted than ever. He suddenly felt tired, even dizzy, as the adrenaline surged.

He certainly didn't feel in the right frame of mind to discuss his future with Maggie Ferguson.

But he had to.

He stood in front of Maggie's door, hand raised in a fist, about to knock and call time on his hugely enjoyable stint in London.

And then his phone rang.

It was Sarah.

Cullen moved away from the door and back into the stairwell. He felt relief at his stay of execution. But the feeling was short-lived.

'Paul,' Sarah said. 'Are you able to talk?'

She was upset.

'Yes, yes, of course. What's the matter?'

'It's Philip...'

Cullen remained in the brightly lit stairwell, the looming discussion with Maggie Ferguson now faded into the background.

'What's the matter?' he asked, trying to suppress the anxiety he was feeling as a result of the unexpected call.

Cullen knew that for Sarah to call during office hours, it must be very bad news about his friend and brother-in-law, Philip, the former rugby league international who for the past few years had been battling the devastating illness of early onset dementia.

The illness had robbed Cullen's childhood friend of everything.

And it had also taken something away from Cullen and Sarah.

Cared for in a specialist residential home up in Wigan, it had been the reason for Sarah's move back up North just over six months ago. She'd wanted to be near him, to ensure that he could remain in Acorn House. Philip's increasing outbursts of aggression had seen the home struggling to cope, and Sarah's presence was an effective calming influence on the still man-mountain of a man.

But there was always the risk that he could turn from mild-mannered to violent...

What if he'd done something to hurt one of the staff?

Sarah still hadn't responded.

Cullen tried again, half-thinking that their connection might have been lost. 'Sarah? What's up?'

'He's gone,' she whispered at last.

Cullen caught his breath. 'Gone? He's...'

'The home called me an hour ago,' she began, hesitantly, as if she was still trying to process the information. 'They found him in bed, thought he was still sleeping. But he'd gone.'

Cullen slumped back against the cold concrete wall of the stairwell. He couldn't believe it. Even though Philip had been unwell now for some years, it still came as a shock that the man who had exuded so much life on and off the rugby field was now dead. He longed to reach out and hold his wife. 'Oh, Sarah, I'm so sorry. So sorry.'

Sarah sniffed back tears. 'I'm at Acorn House now,' she explained. 'I've just come outside for some fresh air, take some time to think. They've moved Philip to the chapel room. I went to see him...he looked so...'

Sarah began to sob.

Cullen felt helpless, listening to his wife's grief, raw and painful. 'I love you,' was all that he could think to say. Amazingly it seemed to help, and she quietened almost immediately.

'I love you, too,' she replied. There was a pause. 'They've done things so nicely,' she said. 'Philip looks peaceful. Like he's asleep.'

'Dreaming of the rugby, running in the winning try,' Cullen said, the words catching in his throat. He remembered back to those times, not so long ago, when in front of tens of thousands of screaming fans, Philip would thunder through tackles and burst out of the line, powering to score. 'I can see him now, running around up there.'

Sarah laughed away her sadness. 'Me too.'

'Did they say how they think it happened?' Cullen asked, already knowing that it was too early for answers to those kind of questions. But Philip hadn't shown any signs of physical deterioration recently, and had actually seemed better than he had done in a while just two weeks ago, when Cullen had visited.

He remembered giving his friend a big hug.

Not knowing it would be for the last time.

Cullen swallowed away the tears that were bubbling away underneath.

Just then the top door to the stairwell swung open and Cullen was surprised to see Maggie Ferguson standing there, looking down towards him.

'Everything okay?' she mouthed.

Cullen cupped a hand across the receiver. 'Bad news from home,' he said.

'Sorry to hear that,' she said. She smiled kindly. 'Can I do anything to help?'

'Maybe,' he replied. 'Thank you.'

Maggie nodded, before returning back through the door towards her office. She was a fearsome operator, and a Boss who certain did not suffer fools. But that didn't mean that she wasn't compassionate. Maggie did care for her staff, she had empathy, Cullen could see that, and that as much as her steeliness was an ingredient in her success.

Cullen returned to the call. 'Sorry about that - Maggie Ferguson,' he explained.

'I'm really sorry for interrupting your work,' Sarah said.

'Oh, no, don't be silly. Something like this, it can't wait - it shouldn't wait.'

'Your question, they think it's just a natural progression of the dementia. They said it might have been his heart, but they just don't know yet.'

'Of course.'

'But they do think it was peaceful,' she added. 'When they found him in the bed, he was in the same position as they left him, tucked up. So there hadn't been any struggling, which I guess means he didn't suffer at all. I think he'd just slipped away.'

'That's good. That's really good. He deserved that, after everything he's been through.'

'Yes.'

A silence descended as Cullen thought on his next move.

'I want to be with you,' he said, before he had time to really think things through. 'I can be with you by mid afternoon.'

There was a moment's hesitation. 'But work...'

'Let me deal with that,' he said, wondering whether Maggie would allow him the grace of the afternoon off. But he was about to do her a big favour, so maybe she would cut him some slack.

'Thank you,' Sarah said simply. 'I could really do with you here.'

11

Present Day

Once the call to Sarah had ended, Cullen took a minute on the stairwell to digest the news of Philip's death. It would take time to process that his best friend had gone, he knew that, and there would be difficult days and weeks ahead. But for now he just had to keep it together.

He didn't want to lose it in front of the Boss.

A sharp knock, followed by a call to enter, saw Cullen once again facing Maggie Ferguson. She was already standing, as if readying herself for the news of the phone call, and her face was softer than usual.

'Is everything okay?' she asked, still professional but with a definite softer edge.

'It's my brother-in-law,' he said. 'Died this morning.'

'I'm very sorry to hear that,' she replied, moving around the desk and perching on the front in a display of informality that Cullen had not seen before from her. 'Was it...expected?'

'Yes...and no.'

'Would you like to talk about it?'

Maggie knew about the situation, given the impact that Philip's illness had had on Cullen's family life in the past few months. But he updated her on things, how Philip had seemed bright a few weeks earlier, and that his death had been sudden but apparently peaceful.

She listened and nodded. 'My mother suffered from dementia,' she said, when Cullen had finished. 'Came on in her early sixties. She was such a bright, busy woman. But afterwards, well,' she smiled sadly, 'she wasn't. And sometimes she knew it...she knew what she had lost, somehow she knew. So I know how hard it can be for the family, and the person themselves. When the end came, it was a mixture of relief and grief.'

Cullen tried to hide his surprise. This was the first time Maggie had revealed their family had also been touched by dementia.

'I never knew,' he said. 'Sorry to hear that.'

He felt strangely let down that she hadn't shared this until now. But it did explain why she had always been accommodating on the issue, allowing Cullen leeway on time off relating to Sarah's move back up to Wigan for example. Maybe it would work in his favour now.

'I try not to share my personal troubles with others,' she replied. 'Maybe that's a mistake...I don't know.'

'I don't know either,' Cullen admitted. 'I used to think I kept my personal and professional life separate, but I'm not sure I can say that anymore.'

That elicited a knowing smile from Maggie. 'Well I'd just say, keep on doing what you're doing, Paul. You're popular with your team, and successful in your role; this place would be much weaker without you.'

'Thank you,' Cullen said, taken aback by the rare praise. Maggie Ferguson did give positive feedback, but it was never usually delivered quite so directly and fulsomely.

'So what now?' she said. 'You want to be with Sarah, I'm sure.'

Cullen nodded. 'I was hoping...'

'Go,' Maggie said. 'Get the next train up there, and that's an order.'

'Are you sure?'

'I'm sure Danny can hold the fort for the rest of the day,' she replied. 'Just make sure he's okay with it on your way out.'

'Thank you. There are things I can work on, on the train up there.'

'I'm sure there are. Or just stare out of the window and think about the good times with your brother-in-law.'

Cullen nodded.

Maggie went to speak, then checked herself. Finally she spoke, but with some hesitation. 'The sleeper train this Friday,' she said. 'Is that still okay for you?'

'Yes,' Cullen said without missing a beat. He knew the score. Ferguson had cut him some slack now, and he would repay the favour this coming weekend. As much as he didn't particularly want to do it, it was his professional duty, not a holiday break.

'Thank you,' Maggie Ferguson said, with more gratitude than Cullen had expected. 'I know it's not ideal under the circumstances, but I really do appreciate it.'

'No problem.'

Maggie Ferguson nodded, then suddenly remembered the genesis of their meeting. 'You wanted to speak to me about something?'

Even Cullen had forgotten that by now. 'It's nothing,' he waved away, 'nothing that can't wait.'

Over the past ten minutes the ground had shifted, and the future which had suddenly seemed so clear, was now much less so.

It was not the time for making life-changing decisions.

Not yet.

12

Present Day

CULLEN CHECKED in downstairs with Danny, who was more than happy to pick up the rest of the day as lead to allow Cullen's early journey back up to the North West. By the time he was ready to leave the office, he'd received several heart-warming messages of support from members of the team, as news spread quickly.

They really were a great group.

En route to the hotel where he continued to live during the working week, Cullen called Sarah with the news that he would be with her by the early afternoon. There was an express service leaving London Euston at eleven thirty, which would speed him to Wigan in just under two hours. He'd said he could get a taxi over to Acorn House, but Sarah had insisted that she'd prefer to pick him up from the station.

The time was tight, so Cullen worked quickly at the hotel, stuffing in toiletries and clothes into the small bag. He reached Euston with a few minutes to spare, hopping onto the train and settling down at an empty table in first class. Free first class train travel was one of the few perks of the job with the British Transport Police, and it helped with being able to work during the journey.

But as Maggie Ferguson had suggested, Cullen did little constructive work over the next two hours. The one exception was taking a call from Danny, who reported the pleasantly surprising news that Hampshire had agreed to increase their support in the effort to catch the Masked Mugger. It was not as much as they had asked for, but still a step in the right direction.

Before and after Danny's call, Cullen gazed out at the countryside that flashed past, thinking back to those early days with Philip, when they had laughed and joked their way through hard but rewarding junior and then senior rugby seasons. They had been the best of times, with little responsibility and so much potential ahead of them.

There was that saying, that youth is wasted on the young, and how true that was.

What he would give to get those times back, even for a short while, and relive the feeling. To chat and laugh with his friend, and talk about everything and nothing with the war wounds from the game still raw and throbbing.

Dreams of returning to the past were both fruitless and pointless.

But maybe it was a necessary part of the grieving process, replaying the tape and bathing in the memories, soothing and healing the pain of the present loss.

Cullen allowed himself to remain in his wistful state until they reached the outskirts of the town. The train came to a smooth stop and he stepped out onto the platform to see

Sarah waiting for him. The blustery wind played with her hair as they embraced and the train departed towards Edinburgh.

Sarah buried her head in Cullen's sizeable frame and, wordless, they held one another tightly.

Finally they parted to face one another. Sarah was crying and Cullen trapped a tear on her cheek.

'I'm so glad you're here,' she said.

'Me too.'

Hand in hand, they descended the steps down towards the car park and twenty minutes later, with Cullen driving, they arrived at Acorn House.

~

'Are you okay?' Sarah asked, as they approached the chapel room. The nurse who had welcomed them on arrival had just left, with the promise that should they need anything she would be just down the corridor. 'You sure you're ready to do this?'

Cullen nodded, although he really didn't feel that sure at all. It wasn't the thought of seeing a dead body - his job had necessitated that many times, and in much more traumatic circumstances - it was the fact that this wasn't just anyone.

It was his childhood friend.

Philip. Full of life. But no longer.

'As long as you're sure,' Sarah said.

Cullen gripped her hand and mustered a smile. 'I want to see him.'

They stepped into the candle-lit room, which did resemble a chapel, with its red carpeted floor and ornate furniture. It smelled of roses, which was a relief, given that

Cullen had a real dislike of the strong scent of lilies, the often-used flower of funerals.

Philip was lying on his back, on a special table in the centre of the room. They'd dressed him smartly, in trousers and his favourite Wigan rugby polo shirt, and it looked like he was catching a few winks before going out on the town.

'He does look very peaceful,' Cullen commented.

Sarah nodded at his side, bitting down on her bottom lip.

Cullen brought a hand around Sarah's back. 'I still can't believe it,' he said. 'That he's gone.'

'I know.'

'He looks powerful,' Cullen noted, surprised by his friend's appearance. The dead often did not quite resemble the living version - the result of the body having shut down, the blood no longer pumping, the skin changing. Seeing the visual change in loved ones was often a shock for relatives faced with death, with the frequent response that they no longer looked like themselves.

But it was different here. Philip appeared to have been enhanced, transformed back into the person he had been - his six foot five inch frame almost God-like in its majesty.

'I know what you mean,' Sarah replied at last. 'He seems...'

'Healed,' Cullen finished.

'Yes, somehow,' she said.

They both took in the sight for a minute or more. Cullen wondered if Philip was looking on now, smiling at the two of them as they paid their respects to what was now just an empty shell. Cullen wasn't a religious man, but his childhood Catholic roots although now largely withered, lived on in his belief that there could be something more.

'I'm sorry,' Cullen said to his fallen friend, breaking the silence.

Sarah looked across in confusion. 'Sorry for what?'

'For everything that happened to him,' he explained. 'For everything he lost, everything that got taken away from this great man.'

'But that's not your fault.'

Cullen reached out and touched Philip's cold hand. 'I could have done more,' he said, referring to how he had distanced himself from Philip in those first few years as the dementia had really taken hold. It was still a source of guilt, and more so again now, how he had abandoned in his friend - and Sarah - in their hour of need.

'You had your reasons. But later, you were there for him,' she said. 'That's what matters. You can't beat yourself up over the past - Philip wouldn't want that.'

Cullen nodded as Sarah squeezed his other hand. He'd stayed away because he was scared of facing not only the reality of what was happening to his friend - how it had utterly robbed him of himself - but also the fear of it happening to himself. Philip's early onset of dementia had been linked to the countless, thunderous hits he had received on the rugby field. And for many years, although not to Philip's professional level, Cullen had experienced the same trauma. Who knew what effect that had on his brain?

But as Sarah had said, he had turned things around, and re-entered Philip's life, to make things good. And for that, Cullen would be forever grateful.

'You made him happy, these last six months,' Sarah added as a further attempt at comfort, 'I could see it.'

'You made me happy too,' Cullen directed at Philip. 'I'll really miss you, mate.'

13

Present Day

THE NEXT MORNING Cullen woke early with the sun streaming through the curtains and Sarah beside him. He shifted in the bed for a few minutes, trying to grab some extra minutes of rest, but couldn't fall back into slumber. Giving up he took a shower before breakfasting downstairs, preparing the table for Sarah's arrival. This wasn't his house, but it was now the closest thing to a family home they had, given that his other place of residence was a London hotel room.

They'd sold their home down south, and moved most of the stuff into storage.

Sarah had been staying in Philip's house for the past six months, and actually part-owned it - an arrangement that Philip was keen to sort out at the outset of his diagnosis in an attempt to prevent the state from using it to fund his care. Now it would become Sarah's, and maybe Cullen's too, although there was a lot to think about where the future was concerned.

Cullen tore at a second piece of toast and gulped down some strong coffee. Sarah entered, still in her pyjamas, and cheekily grabbed the other half of the toast for herself with just a winning smile in compensation.

'How did you sleep?' she asked.

'Surprisingly well,' Cullen replied. 'Do you want some more toast?' he asked, already feeding another slice of bread into the toaster.

'Thanks,' she replied. 'I slept well too. I didn't think I would.'

'Probably all the emotional energy,' Cullen said. 'It takes it out of you.'

Sarah nodded. 'Must be why I'm so hungry,' she replied, reaching across for the cereals.

Cullen handed her a freshly made cup of tea - Sarah couldn't stand coffee. 'I could rustle up a fry up if you like?'

'Or we could go to *Duncan's*? For old time's sake?'

'Good call.' *Duncan's* was a brilliant locally-owned, independent cafe on the outskirts of the town, which did the most amazing breakfasts. Owned by a former Wigan rugby league player, Duncan Edwards, and his wife Cathy, it had been one of Philip's favourite places to eat. During the height of Philip's rugby career, he would polish off their biggest breakfast option with ease, and talk through rugby tactics and form with Duncan - who was never averse to imparting his wisdom gleaned from a career in the all-conquering, dominant Wigan team of the 1980's. 'We'd probably better book,' Cullen mused, 'you know how it gets.'

'Already on it,' Sarah said, grabbing her phone. 'Ten o'clock okay?'

'Perfect.'

'We can combine it with a visit to Haigh Hall.'

A couple of miles outside Wigan, Haigh Hall Country Park overlooked the town from its high vantage point, offering amazing views across the Lancashire countryside. It was a very popular leisure destination, particularly on the weekends, for families, walkers and dog owners, and a regular haunt of Cullen and Sarah.

'Sounds good. We can try and walk off the *Duncan's* breakfast.'

In his younger days, Cullen would often run up to the country park, around and back with Philip and other rugby friends as part of their stamina training. Haigh Hall later became a place of romantic walks with his future wife, and after that a place to let their daughter Amy loose. Amy would love to play on the slides and swings in the park and bathe in the open-air paddling pool.

Haigh Hall was full of the best memories, and a perfect destination for a day like today, particularly with the weather set to be sunny.

'How do you feel this morning?' Cullen asked, taking a seat opposite Sarah. 'Cold light of day, and everything.'

Sarah shrugged. 'It all still feels a bit unreal, I guess. Like it could have just been a dream. But it wasn't, was it?'

Cullen gave a shake of his head. He knew what she meant though.

'I need to get on with the arrangements,' Sarah added. 'The funeral. There's lots to do.'

Sarah was a queen of organisation, and had already contacted the undertakers by the time Cullen had stepped off the platform in Wigan. The firm was one that they were familiar with, and Philip had chosen them himself in those early days of his illness. But that was just the first step, and Sarah had probably by now drawn up a project plan to document each and every step between now and the day of Philip's cremation.

'Anything I can help with, just let me know,' Cullen offered, knowing full well that his role would already have been allocated.

'You're chief word-getting-around person,' she answered without missing a beat. 'Use your contacts, get that church full to the brim.'

'I can do that,' Cullen replied, relieved that Sarah had indeed played to his strengths. 'I've already put the word around a few of the guys via facebook.'

'I've drafted an announcement for the local paper,' Sarah revealed, handing Cullen her phone.

'This is good,' said Cullen, impressed. 'You prepared this beforehand?'

'Wrote it yesterday, just before you arrived.'

'It's perfect,' he added.

'But we can't rely on it to get to everyone, which is why I need your help. We need some publicity.'

'I can arrange a leaflet and poster campaign across the Northern rail network,' Cullen joked.

Sarah smiled. 'I was thinking more of a newspaper story, to go with the announcement.'

Cullen nodded. 'Philip was a big name in the town. I'm sure they'd be happy to run a story. '

'We need it to be front page, for maximum visibility. They can include the details of the service in the story.'

'Front page?'

'Or page two or three,' she conceded, noting Cullen's look. 'Do you think you can manage that?'

It felt like more of an instruction rather than a question. Cullen was up for the challenge.

He'd done this kind of thing before, with impressive results.

'Leave it to me.'

~

JUST BEFORE HEADING out for their second breakfast, while Sarah was showering, Cullen fired a text off to Zack Carter, the journalist from the London Daily Post who he had struck up a positive rapport with during the search for Natalie Long.

Zack was originally from St. Helens, the neighbouring town just a few miles away, and although now based in the capital Cullen remembered that the young reporter had mentioned working for the Wigan News not so long ago. If he could suggest a contact at the newspaper, or even better put in a good word, they might get their featured story on Philip.

Cullen was surprised when, within less than a minute, his phone rang with Zack's number showing on the display.

Cullen put down the bowl that he was in the middle of rinsing. 'Zack, I didn't expect such a speedy response.'

'Detective Cullen,' Zack replied, 'you caught me at a good time. I was just about to hit the track.'

'Running?'

'Racing. Karting to be precise - our weekly league. I just got your text before the warm up laps, and I thought, well there's no time like the present.'

'I appreciate it,' Cullen said, thinking back to the one time he had been karting, back in Wigan with Philip and some of the rugby lads. It had all got a bit too competitive and he'd spun off the track when several karts had come together at high speed, nearly doing himself a nasty injury. 'So, can you help me out?'

'I certainly can,' he replied confidently. 'The Deputy Editor is a good friend of mine - Harry McMillan. He's also a big Wigan rugby supporter, so you're pushing at an open door there. He might have been planning a feature story anyway. Oh, sorry, I meant to start by saying, I'm really sorry to hear about your friend.'

'Thank you,' Cullen said, 'he was a good man. Which is why we want to ensure that people know where they can pay their respects.'

'Sure. I can put a call through to Harry. Is it okay if I pass on your number? It will probably be tomorrow by the time he gets back to you.'

'Of course. And yes, feel free to do that. Do stress how much I'd appreciate it.'

'I will.'

Cullen heard Sarah exiting the bathroom. She would be impressed at the speed of his success. 'That's great, Zack, much appreciated. Speak at some point in the...'

'There was one more thing,' Zack interrupted.

'Go on...'

A pause. 'It's about Daniel Deep.'

'Daniel Deep?' Cullen was taken aback. Surely this was about the upcoming sleeper train trip? But how on earth did Zack know about it, given that it was only just over twenty-four hours since Cullen had agreed to it? He decided not to make assumptions. 'I'm not sure what you mean.'

'Oh,' Zack replied, hesitant and possibly disappointed. 'I'd heard that you would be travelling with him this weekend, up to Scotland on his new sleeper service.'

So he did know.

'You heard correct.' Cullen didn't see any point in denying it. But he did want some answers, as he didn't like to think of the press being briefed on his movements - particularly so soon after he'd actually found out himself. 'How do you know?'

'Because I'll be on the train too', he revealed, much to Cullen's surprise.

'Really?'

'We were contacted by Daniel Deep's people a few weeks ago, and asked to lead on the press reporting for the inaugural journey. He wanted someone on board to write a feature piece that will then be syndicated globally - his team have set up connections across the world with various publications across the States, Europe and Asia. It's all pretty exciting, and a massive opportunity for me at the stage of my career.'

Booking on-board press and a globally syndicated news feature. This certainly wasn't meant to be a low-key event, which was fine, as long as Cullen could keep in the background. 'Sounds like a fantastic opportunity, Zack,' he agreed. 'It's also a big vote of confidence in you, that your employers at the *Post* put your name forward for such a high profile assignment.'

'They didn't.'

'Oh?'

'Daniel Deep requested me personally,' he said, laughing in continued disbelief. 'His team wanted me to do it. They called with my name, and wouldn't accept anyone else, despite a few of the seniors making their case. It caused a bit of an issue actually, but, you know, they wanted me.'

'That's interesting,' Cullen said, reflecting on the similarity to what had happened with him and the hand-picked nature of his involvement with the sleeper train. 'How did he know about you?'

'According to his team, he's read a few of my articles while he's been down in London, and was impressed. He looked me up on the net, and wanted to give a young journalist a chance. It's all a bit mind-blowing still, to be honest; Deep is such a global name, a billionaire, and to think he not only knows who I am but wants me to do this work is just wonderful, but also weird.'

'Well it's definitely a massive opportunity,' Cullen repeated. 'I've heard he's quite a character.'

'Yes, he is. And in a bit of a sticky situation, too.'

'With his behaviour - the sackings?' Cullen ventured, thinking back to what Danny had told him of his ruthless acquisition and destruction of competitors.'

'I mean the incident in the States a few weeks ago. The derailment.'

'Derailment?'

'He runs a rail freight company,' Zack said, confirming what Maggie Ferguson had told him. 'Five weeks ago, in Kansas, a massive train derailed and burst into flames, just outside the town of Hope. The train was carrying a range of harmful chemicals, and the smoke carried them across the town. There's a big bust-up between the residents, the US authorities and Daniel Deep, about supposed health impacts on the people and animals. Local people have reported breathing difficulties, death of livestock, pollution of the local watercourse, while Deep supposedly isn't having any of it.'

Another strong indication of Deep's less than pleasant persona. 'I hadn't heard about that.'

Danny hadn't mentioned anything about a train crash,

and Cullen hadn't spotted any stories covering the incident in his quick Google search.

'Not really been reported in this country,' Zack confirmed. 'And a lot of the media internationally have connections with Deep, so it didn't gain traction, if you catch my meaning.'

'Understood. So how did you know I was also going to be on board?' Cullen probed, returning to his initial question.

'I've got access to the live guest list,' he revealed. 'And your name was confirmed yesterday around lunchtime.'

'I see.' Maggie certainly hadn't wasted any time in informing Deep's people that they had their police officer. She must have called them straight away.

'You were the last to confirm,' Zack added. 'Fashionably late,' he joked.

'I wasn't playing hard to get, I only got the invite yesterday,' Cullen revealed.

'Really?'

'Maybe my Boss was thinking through whether to ask me,' Cullen wondered out loud.

Or maybe she wanted to give him less time to change his mind.

'Maybe.'

'So you know exactly who's going to be onboard?'

'Yes. I'm sure Deep's people will let you know who the fellow guests are.'

Cullen took the hint and didn't press for any more information. He probably wouldn't recognise the names anyway.

'It's funny,' Zack added, 'how you and I have been been singled out for this.'

'Yes,' Cullen agreed, musing on that fact. 'That's one word for it.'

14

Present Day

PROFESSOR BRODY WAS ALREADY SEATED and eating by the time Curtis arrived at the diner.

'These eggs are just so delicious,' Brody said, forking in a mouthful and then washing it down with a slurp of coffee.

Curtis took a seat as Brody swallowed the food and drink.

'Sorry I'm late,' Curtis began. 'Overslept.'

It was the truth. He'd only got to bed around three am, unable to settle his mind after the decision he had made. So when he'd finally succumbed to sleep, he'd gone right through until nine, giving him only half an hour to get up and travel across to the diner.

'It's fine, it's fine,' the Professor waved away with his fork. 'You had a big night last night, a good night. You deserved a lie in.'

Curtis nodded, the shame eating away at his gut as the young waitress, Jessica, came to take his order.

'Just a black coffee for me,' he said.

The Professor looked up in surprise as Jessica returned to the counter.

'Not hungry?'

'Had something before I left,' Curtis lied. In truth, his appetite had deserted him and even the saliva-inducing smells coming from the kitchen were unable to turn things around.

Brody nodded. 'I guess you can eat in this joyous place whenever you like, whereas I need to take my chances.'

Curtis sipped at his strong coffee and watched the Professor finish off his full cooked breakfast. He didn't want to say what he had to say while the guy was still eating. Best to let the Professor enjoy it, wait until the table was clear, and then he would do what he needed to do.

And do it as fast as he could.

'I've been thinking,' Curtis began, once the plate had been taken away. 'About the whole legal thing, taking the case against Deep Distribution. I don't think it's a good idea.'

Brody nodded, not actually looking shocked.

'You're not surprised?'

Brody smiled. 'I've lost count of the number of communities I've worked with on issues like this. I've been around the block and back again, many times. Nothing really surprises me these days.'

'I guess,' Curtis said, feeling a sense of relief that this might be a lot easier than he had feared.

'Tell me your reasoning, Curtis. Let's talk it through. And remember, I'm not here with my own agenda; I'm here because you asked for my help. And you were prepared to pay me for it, of course.'

Jessica came over and refilled their drinks.

'You tell me you don't need me anymore, and I'll be out of here, absolutely no hard feelings. My belly is full and my wallet not empty, at least. But before I do hit the highway, my job is to make sure you're making the right decision, and for the right reasons.'

Curtis swallowed, readying himself for the lies. 'I just think it's all too much,' he began. 'The town, the community, we need to focus on the future, move on from this. Taking Deep Distribution through the courts, it just feels too much, and potentially destructive and confrontational. And we could do all that and still lose. But if we work in partnership with the company, without resorting to legal threats, it's a more positive way forward.'

Brody took on board what he'd just heard. 'That's quite different to what you said yesterday,' he stated simply.

'I've had time to think about it,' Curtis replied.

Brody hesitated, distracted by something over Curtis's shoulder, before his gaze returned to his coffee. 'They've got to you, haven't they?' he said, looking back at Curtis.

Curtis shook his head, but could feel himself redden. 'I don't know what...'

'There's a man on the far side of the diner,' Brody explained. 'He's been watching us. I've seen him before. He did some work for the oil company in Nebraska, passive aggressive stuff, tried to persuade people to drop their legal action.'

Curtis tensed. The man was there to watch them, to make sure that Curtis stuck to his side of the deal.

Had he somehow known about the breakfast meeting with Professor Brody?

Or had the man been following him or the Professor?

Whichever explanation, it was equally chilling.

'I've made my decision,' Curtis said, not responding openly to the news of the man's presence.

Professor Brody leant in closer. 'It's very intimidating, I know, most unpleasant; they specialise in doing this to people. But I can help. The people of Grangetown, I helped them and they resisted and won.'

'It's not the same here.'

'It's never the same.'

'I'm sorry,' Curtis said, the fight having left him. 'I've made my decision.'

PART II

15

Previously

DEEP INDUSTRY'S headquarters was an imposing glass-and-steel skyscraper located in the heart of San Francisco's financial district. The building stood at sixty stories, and since its construction five years ago was one of the city's most recognisable landmarks.

The headquarters was designed to exude an air of prestige, power, and success; a symbol of Daniel Deep's unwavering commitment to excellence.

Jack Walker was just returning from lunch, where he had met an old university friend for a coffee and sandwich. The lovely meet-up had been rudely interrupted by a notification to return to the offices as soon as possible, for a meeting with Daniel Deep.

He knew what this was about and had been panicking all the way back.

Jack entered the lobby, with its high ceiling and sleek

modern design, furnished with minimalist black leather seating and contemporary art pieces. As with the rest of the building, natural and artificial lighting was carefully calibrated to create a bright and energising work environment. The large, polished marble reception desk was, as usual, manned by a team of impeccably dressed receptionists who greeted visitors and employees warmly.

Except that Jack didn't feel able to return their smiles.

He approached the elevators, which were banked in a row, whisking guests and employees alike to their destinations with minimal waiting time. The building contained countless offices, conference rooms, and breakout areas designed with a modern and minimalist aesthetic, with each floor dedicated to a different company owned by Daniel Deep.

With a strong sense of trepidation, Jack stepped inside the lift and travelled up towards the top floor.

~

DANIEL DEEP PACED ANGRILY in his office, his eyes narrowing as he glared at the trembling employee before him. The employee, a young man named Jack, looked down at his feet, clearly terrified.

Deep enjoyed cultivating his cold and callous demeanour, exuding his air of superiority and entitlement. Through a carefully calculated mixture of harsh and degrading language, he enjoyed belittling his employees, making them feel small and insignificant. It was fun to play with words and body language, to see how much they would take before walking - if he gave them the option to stay, that is.

'Jack, do you have any idea what you've done?' Deep

sneered. 'The shipment was delayed, and now we're going to miss our deadline. I trusted you to handle this, and you let me down.'

Deep had done this countless times before, using his position of power to make unreasonable demands and set impossible goals, then berating the employee when they failed to meet his expectations.

He took pleasure in humiliating his employees, in order to assert his dominance and maintain his control over them.

Jack's face went pale. 'I'm sorry, Mr. Deep. There were unforeseen circumstances, I..'

'Unforeseen circumstances?' Deep interrupted, his voice rising in anger. 'I don't want excuses, Jack. I want results. And now you're fired.'

Jack's shoulders slumped, and he hung his head in defeat. 'But Mr Deep, please. It wasn't entirely my fault. I did everything I could...'

'Enough!' Deep shouted. 'I don't want to hear it. You're a liability to this company, and I won't tolerate incompetence. You can collect your things and leave immediately.'

Jack nodded silently, his eyes welling up with tears as he turned to leave. Deep watched him go, feeling a sense of satisfaction at having put the employee in his place.

As Jack walked out of the office, Deep leaned back in his chair, feeling a sense of power and control wash over him.

16

Present Day

PAUL CULLEN STEPPED off the tube train, travel bag in hand, still irked from the lack of direction he'd received, regarding his policing role onboard Deep Sleeper.

The personable but ultimately frustrating lady he had spoken to on the phone two days' ago had said that he'd receive instructions upon his arrival at the station. Cullen had protested that leaving it so late wasn't really acceptable, but this had only led to a polite apology from the woman who had introduced herself as Emily Parker, Daniel Deep's Personal Assistant.

'I'm really sorry, Detective, but all will become clear on Friday evening,' she had promised.

Still thinking back to that conversation and how uncharacteristically unprepared he felt for the job to come, he moved through the crowds towards the main part of London King's Cross station.

Emerging onto the busy concourse, with the time just turning eight o'clock in the evening, Cullen was met with echoing announcements over the loudspeaker and people with hurried footsteps criss-crossing to their destinations. The sights and sounds lifted his spirits; he always loved a busy train station - all that movement and energy. His detective instincts keenly observing his surroundings, Cullen made his way through the bustling crowd and towards the VIP waiting room.

As he approached the entrance to the VIP area, he was met by a smartly-dressed attendant. Wearing a crisp, bright blue uniform with a Deep Sleeper logo emblazoned on the lapel, the man in his twenties extended a welcoming hand as he held a tablet computer against his side.

'Detective Cullen, I presume?' the attendant asked with a warm smile as he proffered a white gloved hand.

'Do I look that much like your stereotypical police detective?' Cullen quipped.

The man grinned. 'We have all your photos on here,' he said, lifting up the tablet. 'My job is to know who each and every one of the twenty guests are, including what they look like.'

Cullen nodded. 'Well, you got me.' He finally shook the man's hand. 'Paul Cullen, British Transport Police.'

'Lovely to meet you, Inspector. I know Mr Deep was so delighted that you were able to accept his invitation to join this inaugural journey as one of his very special guests.'

'I thought it was more of a job,' Cullen replied. 'Train security.'

'I'm sure Mr Deep will explain everything, once you board,' he replied, dodging the question. 'Now, Inspector,' he continued, before Cullen could enquire further, 'please, follow me through into the lounge.'

Cullen followed, as the attendant led him to a set of grand double doors adorned with polished brass handles. As the doors swung open, Cullen's eyes widened in awe at the sight before him.

'This area has been created especially for Deep Sleeper,' the attendant explained, 'to Mr Deep's personal specification.'

The VIP waiting room was a spacious, lavishly decorated lounge. Soft lighting illuminated the room, casting a warm and inviting ambiance. Plush leather armchairs and sofas, already populated by fellow passengers, were arranged in small conversational clusters, while elegant coffee tables showcased fresh floral arrangements that were the obvious source for the welcoming scent. The walls were adorned with tasteful artwork, capturing scenic landscapes and famous London landmarks.

'Very impressive,' Cullen commented. If this was the standard that they were to expect on the rest of their weekend, it had the potential to be very pleasant indeed. He felt a pang of guilt at the thought of Sarah, back in Wigan, preparing for the funeral.

'Champagne?' a voice asked.

Cullen turned and was handed a flute before he'd had chance to think. He thanked the girl, who had already moved away with the tray full of drinks.

'I'll leave you here, Detective,' the attendant said. 'I do hope you have a lovely journey.'

Cullen took a tentative sip from the champagne as the man left him alone. He looked across at the other passengers - or very important guests - not quite knowing how or who to engage. He caught a few glances coming his way, and feeling increasingly self-conscious, was relieved when he saw Zack approach.

'Zack, great to see you,' he said, as they did a friendly backslap that seemed a little out of keeping for the surroundings.

'You too, Detective,' Zack said. 'I see you're already getting in the swing of it,' he noted, gesturing at the drink.

'Y-e-s,' Cullen replied. 'Not usually one for the fizzy stuff, but, you know.'

'When in Rome?'

'Something like that.'

'So, looking forward to this?' Zack asked.

Cullen shrugged. 'I still don't know what my role is,' he said. 'I've asked, but they said I'll find out when I board. All very strange. I don't like it. You don't know anything more?'

Zack shook his head. 'Sorry. But I do know though who these people are. Would you like me to introduce you to a few of them?'

'I'm feeling a little anti-social,' Cullen admitted. 'To be honest, I'm already looking forward to hitting the sack.'

Zack laughed. 'I'm sure you'll get into the spirit.'

'Possibly,' Cullen conceded. 'So, maybe give me a quick summary of who these people are.'

Zack nodded. 'There are twenty special guests on board, including us two. I've been keeping count, and this is everyone now.'

'You mean I was last?'

'Not as desperate for the complimentary drinks and canapés,' Zack joked. 'Just Daniel Deep to go.'

'He's not here yet either?'

'Arriving any moment, but straight onto the train. Once he's settled, we'll be boarding.'

'I see.'

Cullen watched as a group at one of the tables quaffed back the champagne and savoured bites of hors d'oeuvres served by the attentive waiters. The food didn't really appeal to Cullen's working class, Wigan tastebuds. 'So who are those guys?'

Zack spoke softly, trying to not make it obvious what he was doing. He went through the basic biographical details of each of the guests with ease, without any notes as a reminder. They were almost all American businesspeople, mostly from the tech sector, with a few exceptions; a man engaged in an animated conversation with one of the waitresses was revealed to be Daniel Deep's cousin, while a lady in the group that Cullen had scrutinised was a Senator.

All were dressed uber-smart, with the men in suits and women in expensive looking outfits.

With one exception.

'Who's that guy?' Cullen asked, nodding as subtly as he could at the bearded, bespectacled man standing on his own in the far corner of the room. Unlike the others, he was dressed casually, in slightly too baggy red corduroy trousers, a grey jumper and fisherman-style bright yellow jacket. Cullen really liked the look of him.

'Oh, that's Professor Ben Brody. He's an interesting one. Specialist in environmental disaster management; one of the best in the world. Has worked on lots of cases where communities have been affected by environmental incidents, and has helped them win against some very big companies. You remember I mentioned to you about the accident in the

States recently, involving Deep Distribution, with the derailment and explosion?'

'The town called Hope, wasn't it?' The ironic name had stuck with him.

'Yes, that's the one. Well, Professor Brody was involved in representing the community.'

'Against Daniel Deep? And now he's a guest on his train?' It sounded weird at best, and suspicious at worst.

'Strange, I know. And the Prof, he's not someone to be turned to the dark side, believe me - when I found out he was on the trip, I researched him to death. He's a straight-up good guy, very ethically driven, principles running through him like a stick of Blackpool Rock.'

Cullen smiled at the memories-laden analogy. He'd spent many an enjoyable childhood trip, and several more when his daughter Amy had been little, at the famous northern seaside resort. 'I'd definitely like to talk to Professor Brody.'

'Let's do it then,' Zack said, making to approach the Professor, who was fiddling with his mobile phone. 'There's something else I need to speak to you about,' Zack added, as they crossed the room.

Cullen paused.

'Something a bit weird about the guest list, or at least, interesting,' Zack continued in hushed tones.

'Go on,' Cullen prompted, his interest piqued.

'It might be nothing, but...'

Zack was interrupted by the tinkling of a glass, which cut the conversation in the room stone dead with impressive effectiveness.

'Ladies and gentlemen,' a lady announced wearing the now familiar blue uniform. 'I am delighted to inform you that Deep Sleeper is ready for boarding. If you will please follow my colleague here, he will direct you to the train. On behalf of Deep Sleeper Experiences, I would like to wish you a very memorable journey.'

As the guests stood as one, and they all edged out of the room, Cullen couldn't help but feel a sense of curiosity and anticipation himself. He knew that whatever happened, and whatever role he was to play, the journey aboard Deep Sleeper would be unlike anything he had experienced before.

As he eyed the other passengers, with his imagination running away from him following Zack's interrupted comment, Cullen was reminded again of Agatha Christie's most famous novel.

This might not have been the Orient Express, but Cullen couldn't help but wonder what secrets, ambitions and motivations lay hidden beneath the guest's polite smiles and their host's mysterious agenda.

17

Present Day

THE GUESTS MADE their way across the station concourse, and were led through an open ticket barrier onto the platform. Cullen walked at Zack's side, unspeaking; he would pick up the conversation about the guest list with the journalist later, when there weren't so many fellow passengers around.

Deep Sleeper was waiting for them. Cullen had seen the promotional images of the locomotive, but it was still an impressive sight in person. The engine, maroon with gold trim, was a powerful American freight train, and behind it, ten heritage style carriages, certainly reminiscent of the Orient Express. At the middle of the train was a domed observation car.

'She's a beauty, isn't she?' Zack noted, as the attendant who had been leading them through the station stopped and waited for the line of passengers to assemble. In front of them were a group of staff with their Deep Sleeper uniforms, ready to greet and assist with boarding.

'Impressive,' Cullen agreed. The promotional material had promised that Deep Sleeper was the height of luxury, with every amenity a passenger could want. He believed it.

One by one, the guests were directed to the right doors for their allocated cabins. Zack was led off first, to the second to last carriage. Now his turn, Cullen was given his instructions before he made his way along to the middle of the train and stepped on board, taking in the opulent surroundings as the smell of vanilla hit him. The walls were lined with rich mahogany panelling, and even in the vestibule area the train was spacious, with plenty of head room for even Cullen and his six foot four inch frame to move around.

'Your room is just down the corridor,' one of the attendants who was waiting for him on board informed him. 'Would you like me to show you to your room, Inspector?'

'It's okay, thank you,' Cullen replied, still marvelling at the luxurious surroundings. The plush carpet and elegant panelled walls made him feel as though he was stepping back in time, to an era of opulent train travel that had long since passed. He had to hand it to Daniel Deep, the guy knew how to design a luxury train.

As he unlocked the door to his cabin and stepped inside, Cullen was struck by the size of the room. It wasn't like your average sleeper train. To the left was a double bed, dressed in crisp white linens. To the right was a small but inviting sofa chair with table, and an internal door led into the en suite luxurious bathroom with its marble accents and high-end fixtures and fittings. The soft glow of the bedside lamps created a warm and inviting ambiance. On the wall was a large flat-screen television and a sound system. Cullen dropped his bag on the luggage rack and peered through the panoramic window to the platform outside. It looked like everyone had boarded. A glance at his watch told him that they would be departing in little over ten minutes. It was all very efficient.

And yet he still hadn't received his assignment.

No sooner had the thought occurred to him, there was a knock on the door.

'Inspector Cullen,' the striking woman with short brown hair and blue eyes said, smiling. Unlike the others, she wasn't in the Deep Sleeper uniform, but was well dressed in a dark suit and pretty blouse. 'I'm Emily; Emily Parker. Daniel's personal assistant. We spoke a few days' ago.'

Cullen shook her hand. 'Pleased to meet you in person.'

'You too, Inspector. I'm here with a message on behalf of Mr Deep. He would like to invite you to dine with him, this evening at nine thirty.'

'He'll tell me more about my role?' Cullen asked, feeling uncomfortable at the continued lack of clarity.

'Yes, he'll explain all then,' she promised.

It still felt inadequate. There was no way he'd expected that the train would have actually set off before he'd be told what he was supposed to be doing. In fact, if he had known that, the high likelihood was that he'd have turned down Daniel Deep's request, no matter how that might have infuriated Maggie Ferguson.

'For now, I'll leave you be, so you can settle down in your cabin,' Emily continued, either ignoring or not noticing Cullen's barely suppressed frustration. 'You may wish to explore the train, of course - I'd recommend the observation car, which is just two carriages down. There's also the restaurant and cocktail bar carriage, towards the front.'

'And that's where I'll be meeting Daniel?'

'Sorry, no, you'll be meeting Mr Deep in his private carriage, which is at the very front of the train. He's very much looking forward to meeting you, Inspector Cullen. He's been planning this trip for months, so I do hope you enjoy it.'

'I'm sure it's going to be quite an experience,' he said cautiously.

'It certainly will be,' said Emily, her tone cryptic. 'Mr Deep has a lot of surprises in store for us.'

As Emily bid him goodbye, Cullen couldn't help but wonder what kind of surprises Daniel Deep had in mind, and if he should be worried. As he settled into his cabin, he couldn't shake the feeling of unease that had settled over him. He knew that Deep had a reputation for being ruthless, and he couldn't help but wonder what the billionaire's motives were in inviting him along.

As Deep Sleeper pulled away from the station, Cullen's unease settled and a thrill of excitement ran through him; not at the thought of spending time on the luxury train or experiencing the rugged beauty of the Scottish Highlands.

But at his detective senses that were tingling.

Mr Deep has a lot of surprises in store for us...

That comment had set him off thinking.

Whatever his role on board, he would need his wits about him; of that he felt certain.

18

Previously

DANIEL DEEP'S home in San Francisco was a stunning example of modern architecture and design, with every detail carefully considered to create a luxurious and comfortable living space. The minimalist masterpiece, nestled in the hills overlooking the city was surrounded by impressive landscaped gardens. Designed at Deep's request by Tomas Hoffmann, the genius German architect, the exterior of the house was a sleek, geometric design, with sharp angles and clean lines, giving it a futuristic feel. The facade, mostly glass, allowed for stunning views of the city skyline and the bay in the distance.

The interior of the house was just as impressive, with high ceilings, polished concrete floors, and a neutral colour palette that accentuated the minimalist aesthetic.

Daniel Deep padded through into the living room, wearing his gym outfit of tightly fitted t-shirt and sweat pants, in preparation for his imminent circuits session with Eric, his personal trainer.

Furnished with stylish, contemporary furniture, the room included a large, modular sofa and an ivory coffee table. The stone walls were adorned with abstract artwork and large, floor-to-ceiling windows offer a breathtaking view of the city.

Deep paused in the centre of the room as he felt a strange sensation in his head; a painful pulse that disappeared as quickly as it arrived. He rarely got headaches, but was probably a little dehydrated after his early morning bike ride around the surrounding hills.

He moved into the kitchen, pouring himself a homemade smoothie from the fridge. He chugged back the thick, green liquid and let out a satisfied noise as it slid down his throat.

The kitchen was a chef's dream, with state-of-the-art stainless steel appliances, an expansive island, and ample counter space for food preparation. He set out to prepare lunch, chopping vegetables with professional precision. When the circuits session was over, he would take a cold shower before enjoying lunch in the dining area, on the long, rustic wooden table with bench seating, surrounded by the floor-to-ceiling windows that offered a stunning view of the cityscape.

Suddenly the head pain was back, this time more stabbing in nature, causing Deep to drop the knife onto the worktop. He pressed into the side of his temple, successfully warding it off.

But as he went to answer the chiming doorbell, echoes of the pain were still bothering him.

19

Previously

Daniel Deep was sitting on a plush cushion on the floor of his private gym, dressed in the tight-fitting fitness outfit that showed off his lean, muscular physique.

How had he achieved such a body?

Thousands of hours of pushing through the pain barrier; in the gym, on the bike around the nearby hills, and his daily wild water swimming.

His strict diet, created bespoke by the world's leading nutritionist.

The vitamin and mineral infusions

And a highly regimented sleep routine.

Deep's body was truly a temple which he worshipped.

Eric, his tall and even more muscular personal trainer, was standing beside him, observing as Deep performed a series of slow, deliberate movements as part of his warm up routine.

Deep's movements were graceful and fluid, yet seemed to have no discernible purpose. He was twisting and bending his body in strange ways, making odd noises and grimacing with effort.

Despite not really understanding Deep's methods, Eric had learned not to question them. He'd heard what had happened to his employer's previous two personal trainers - both let go after daring to challenge Deep's intense approach to health and fitness. He knew one of them, a very experienced former professional ultimate fighter called Cory, who had warned Eric off taking on the role.

Deep is dangerous. Stay away.

But the money had been far too tempting.

Eric watched on without comment, hands on hips. Daniel Deep was a billionaire for a reason, and if these exercises were part of the secret to his success, Eric was happy to play along.

As Deep finished his series of movements, he stood up and began to perform a series of breathing exercises. His eyes were closed, and he appeared to be in a trance-like state.

Then his eyes shot open - so suddenly it actually shocked Eric.

'I'm ready,' Deep said. 'Make this session hard. I want to be pushed to the brink.'

Eric nodded and clapped his hands together, psyching himself up for the challenge.

And it would be a challenge to push this ultra athlete. Deep was as fit as he was demanding.

'Right!' Eric shouted, 'first station, chin ups!'

Deep stalked over to the piece of equipment and leapt up to grip the bar, holding his body weight with ease.

'Thirty seconds!' Eric bawled. 'Go!'

Eric watched, impressed, as Deep pulled himself up and down in rapid, but highly controlled movements.

'Faster!' he cried. 'You can go faster than that.'

Amazingly, Deep did just that.

The timer beeped twice.

'That's it! Next station, bench press. Go!'

Deep jogged across and slid onto the bench, gripping the bar with both hands, awaiting the instruction. His face was full of focus.

'Go!' Eric shouted.

Again, Deep moved fluently and at pace. He was lifting 75kg but made it look easy.

'Harder!'

Again, Deep rose to the challenge.

The thirty seconds over, Deep jumped up, moving from one foot to another like a boxer warming up for a sparring session.

'Too easy,' Deep goaded with a smile. 'You need to work me much harder than this, Eric.'

Eric nodded. 'You bet.' He thought through how he could toughen up the session.

Maybe introduce some heavy free weights?

Or alternate the exercises he had planned with lunges on the crash mat. Now that would surely take it out of even Daniel Deep.

'Crash mat,' Eric ordered.

Deep nodded, seemingly impressed at the surprise choice of activity. He jogged over confidently, but as he neared the mat he thrust both hands to his head, letting out a loud yell as he collapsed to the floor.

'Mr Deep!' Eric shouted, rushing to his employer's side and crouching down. 'Are you okay?'

Deep lay prone on the floor, just short of the crash mat, his body twitching and convulsing and eyes closed. Eric felt a surge of panic rising in his chest. He had no idea what was happening, or what he should do to help.

'Is it a heart attack?' he asked helplessly. 'Epilepsy?'

He rushed across the gym to grab his phone and dialled 911, relaying what was happening in panicked, staccato sentences.

Following the call handler's instructions, and calmed by their voice, he checked Deep's breathing and pulse before putting him in the recovery position.

After what felt like an eternity, Deep's convulsions stopped, and he lay still on the floor. Eric hesitantly reached out to touch his employer's shoulder.

'What's happening to me?' Deep gasped, his hand clutching at his head.

He tried to stand up, but his legs gave out beneath him. Eric caught him and lowered him back to the ground.

'The ringing in my ears,' Deep complained with a grimace.

'It's okay,' Eric said, 'the ambulance is on its way.'

'I don't need an ambulance,' Deep replied, his breathing shallow and laboured. 'Just need a minute to recover...'

But a shooting pain across his temple cut him short.

'You need to rest until the ambulance arrives,' Eric said.

As the ambulance arrived and the paramedics took over, Eric could only watch as Deep was rushed to the hospital, his fate uncertain. He felt sure that something was terribly wrong.

This wasn't just a simple workout injury.

20

Present Day

CULLEN WATCHED the world pass by from his panoramic cabin window, while leafing through the promotional material that the company had left on the coffee table. One leaflet documented the journey they would be taking, pointing out various landmarks of interest. Cullen knew the route already: unlike the long-running Caledonian sleeper service, which left from Euston and took the West Coast Mainline through the Midlands and North West England, Deep's sleeper train would make its way up the east coast from King's Cross station. At a relatively leisurely pace, it would pass through York, Newcastle and Durham, skirting the Northumbrian Coast and North Sea, before entering Scotland and heading for the Highlands.

It would reach its first destination on Saturday morning; the small Highland station of Tulloch. From there they would board a coach for the fifteen minute journey to Daniel Deep's Scottish home, a castle on the banks of Loch Laggan.

Cullen called Sarah for a chat and update, before preparing for his evening meal with Daniel Deep. Deep's personal assistant, Emily had said Deep's carriage was at the very front of the train, beyond the restaurant. He made his way through the train, passing through another carriage of passenger cabins, before reaching the restaurant and bar. He was greeted at the entrance by an employee holding a tablet computer. Beyond him, Cullen could see that the carriage was full of diners, enjoying their luxurious dining experience in what looked like an elegant and sophisticated atmosphere.

'Good evening,' the man said.

Cullen was about to explain that he wasn't here for a table, but the man continued.

'Mr Deep is looking forward to meeting you, Inspector Cullen. Please, follow me.'

Cullen followed him through into the restaurant. As with the rest of the train he had seen so far, the carriage was furnished with plush, comfortable seating and adorned with rich, dark wood panelling. The soft, ambient lighting created a relaxing mood, only interrupted by Cullen's unexpected walkthrough.

He nodded at several of the diners, sitting at the tables that were set with crisp, white linen tablecloths and sparkling silverware. The panoramic windows would no doubt provide breathtaking views of the Scottish Highlands tomorrow at breakfast, but with the light now faded outside, the blinds had come down.

The smell from the food was tormenting Cullen's tastebuds. He'd read in the promotional literature that the menu featured a variety of award winning gourmet dishes, all expertly crafted by the onboard, Michelin-starred chef.

Cullen noticed Professor Brody sitting at the final table, chatting with a companion of whom Cullen could only see the back of their head. He looked up as Cullen passed, with a flash of recognition. 'Detective,' Brody said in greeting.

Cullen's surprise was extinguished when he realised that the Professor's dining companion was Zack. He nodded at them both as he passed, reaching the door on the other side. By this was a bar area, where a bartender was expertly mixing a cocktail.

The corridor narrowed as they continued, with a solid wall on their right.

'The kitchens are behind here,' the man explained over his shoulder, as Cullen followed. 'That's where the culinary magic happens.'

Cullen could feel the heat coming from behind the wall. There couldn't have been much space for the kitchen staff.

'And here we are,' the man announced, after a dog-leg into the next carriage.

They were greeted by a tall, heavily built, suited man, his muscular chest bulging underneath his white shirt. An undoubtably imposing figure, who exuded an air of confidence and authority, the man remained serious when nodding his hello. Cullen spotted the earpiece straight away.

Bodyguard.

Cullen turned to look at the man who had delivered Cullen from the restaurant, but he had left without another word.

'Welcome to Mr Deep's private residence on board Deep Sleeper,' the bodyguard said. He knocked on the door behind him and immediately pushed it open. 'Please, do enter.'

'Thank you,' Cullen replied, stepping through into a private dining room. The table was set in the centre, adorned with more gleaming silver cutlery and crystal glasses, with two empty chairs.

The door closed behind him, while at the very same moment another on the far side swooshed open, and Daniel Deep strode in.

'Detective Chief Inspector Paul Cullen, of the British Transport Police!' Daniel Deep beamed. He strode over and grasped Cullen's hand with both of his, shaking it enthusiastically as if he was greeting a long-lost friend. 'An absolute pleasure to meet you, Detective!'

'Thank you,' was all Cullen could manage, taken aback by the friendly welcome from the individual he had heard and read so much about in the past week.

Deep kept up the shake too long for Cullen's comfort, the athletic looking billionaire smiling at him with his sharp, sculptured features and piercing blue eyes. Finally he snapped out of his thoughts. 'Please, do take a look around my humble abode,' Deep said, his Californian accent strong as he threw his arms up theatrically. 'This is my dining and relaxation area,' he said. 'Which I guess is pretty obvious. The windows are a single pane of glass, to maximise the panoramic view,' he said, gesturing to the external side of the train on his left, which unlike the restaurant carriage did not have the blinds down; although all that could be seen in the darkness was reflections from the lights inside the carriage. 'It frames the wonderful English...and Scottish countryside so beautifully,' Deep added. 'I'm very pleased with how it turned out.'

'It's certainly a very impressive train,' Cullen noted.

That obviously hit the right note. 'Thank you, Detective.

We aim to please. My concept with Deep Sleeper was to create the premier luxury train brand in the world. We're on Deep Sleeper One, but this is just the beginning. Imagine a network of luxury trains, criss-crossing mainland Europe, into Asia, through Russia to China. A service offering the most wonderful experience you could imagine and that will never be forgotten. Just imagine that, Detective Cullen,' he finished, more than a hint of pride in his voice.

'Sounds good.'

The smile on Deep's face faded, as if he had just remembered something bad. 'What do you think of my restaurant?' he said, recovering.

'Well, I haven't tried the...'

'It's a truly exceptional dining experience,' he said. 'The most exquisite food, unparalleled service, and a breathtaking ambiance. My chef, Paulo, is one of the best. And one of the most expensive,' he laughed. 'But worth it. As you will soon find out, when we dine.'

Cullen had been taking in Deep's face while his host had continued to eulogise about his train. Despite both men being of a similar age, Deep's face - unlike Cullen's - was devoid of any wrinkles. Beneath his dyed black hair, Deep's forehead was millpond smooth, his angular, tanned cheeks taut, and lips full. Daniel Deep had certainly kept his cosmetic surgeon busy.

Cullen was just about to ask about his security role, when a member of staff knocked and asked if they were ready for the meal.

They took their seats, while several waiters and waitresses attended to them, bringing out first an asparagus soup starter, followed by the main meal.

'The finest Scottish salmon,' Deep announced, as he

chewed on a bite. 'Fresh from the waters around Loch Laggan. You won't taste a better fish anywhere.'

Cullen had to agree. The food was delicious. But he was still keen to get down to business.

'I wanted to ask about my role on board,' Cullen said, in between mouthfuls. 'My policing duties.'

Deep looked up, a smile seeming to play on his lips.

'It's highly unusual,' Cullen continued, aggravated by Deep's apparent too-relaxed attitude, 'to have been assigned to an official policing duty without any briefing. It feels uncomfortable; even more so now that the train has begun its journey. I would have expected that...'

'I'm so sorry, Detective,' Deep said, cutting across him with sudden seriousness. He placed down his knife and fork. 'I really must apologise for my behaviour. I'm afraid I have got you here under false pretences.'

'I don't understand.'

This guy was impossible to read, with his enhanced, immobile face giving away no obvious ticks.

Yet.

Deep dabbed at his mouth with a napkin before placing it back down on the table. 'There are no official duties for you, Detective,' he revealed.

'But, I was told, the security...'

'Security on Deep Sleeper is all covered,' Deep said, continuing his annoying habit of interrupting. 'You met Karl outside, I presume? He is one of my trusted bodyguards - former US Special Forces, with tours of Afghanistan, Syria and Iraq. There are another couple on board, and more waiting for us at Laggan Castle.'

'I see.' Although in truth, Cullen couldn't really see where this was going, and why he had wasted his time with this if there was no role for him.

'As with Karl, the rest of my security team are a formidable team of highly trained professionals, who are always on high alert to ensure not only my safety and security, but also that of the guests and other staff. Skilled in various forms of self-defence and combat, they are armed with a range of weapons and authorised to use deadly force if necessary.'

'I'm sure that won't be necessary,' Cullen replied, bristling at the realisation that his time had been wasted.

Deep laughed. 'Detective. There are always potential threats when you have the money and profile I have, whether that be physical attacks, kidnapping attempts and even assassination plots. My men are constantly monitoring their surroundings, and are always prepared to act quickly and decisively in order to neutralise any threats.'

'So basically, I won't try anything,' Cullen said, pushing down his continued frustration at this confusing situation.

'Ha!' Deep shouted out with joy, 'I like that, Inspector! I just love the British sense of humour. But seriously, my bodyguards are also trained in diplomacy and conflict resolution, and are skilled in handling any potential altercations in a professional and courteous manner. In short, they give me peace of mind.'

'I can see why you don't need the help of the British Transport Police,' Cullen replied. 'But then why ask for it?'

'Because I wanted you on this journey,' Deep replied without missing a beat. He took a sip of wine. 'I wanted you on Deep Sleeper, and going through the official channels was the most effective way of making that happen.'

'Why me? How do you even know who I am?'

'I just do,' Deep smiled.

Cullen shook his head. That answer wasn't acceptable. 'I'm a lowly police officer with the British Transport Police, Wigan born and raised. You're a billionaire from the west coast of the United States. How you do know me?'

'I feel like I'm under interrogation,' he said, seemingly enjoying the line of questioning. 'But I don't wish to be evasive,' he added. 'It's really nothing that mysterious. I spend a lot of time in the UK, and I'm a huge train fan. I guess you could say I'm obsessed with railways - always have been - and I like to know about them, wherever I am. When I first came to this country, I found out about the British Transport Police, and studied your organisation. I talked to your Mayor about it. And I discovered you, Inspector Cullen, as one of the national leads. I did some homework on you, and liked what I saw. I wanted to meet you.'

'And now you have.'

Deep smiled. 'And now I have. But I want to get to know you much better. I've got a lot of questions!'

It all seemed a bit weird and surreal, but it was starting to make sense, especially when you considered Cullen was dealing with an obviously ego-centric billionaire who was used to having everything he wanted.

Deep reminded Cullen of Kenneth New.

Did great wealth and power do that to people, or did some inherent personality trait drive their attainment of such rewards?

'I am sorry, though,' Deep added. 'Sorry you've been somewhat blindsided by my approach.'

'It's fine,' Cullen replied, choosing to let it lie for the time being, despite feeling aggrieved that Deep's personal desires had stolen a weekend of helping and supporting Sarah through a very difficult time.

He would pick it up next week with Maggie Ferguson, but for now he was on the train, and would just have to roll with the situation.

Deep's bodyguards weren't the only ones who were trained in diplomacy and conflict resolution.

21

Present Day

IT WAS GONE eleven when Paul Cullen left Daniel Deep's suite, exhausted at the intense experience.

'Goodnight, Detective Cullen,' Karl the bodyguard said, as he passed by the man-mountain.

'You too.'

Cullen moved along the corridor back towards the restaurant car, longing for peace in his cabin.The billionaire had asked him question after question about the workings of the British Transport Police - the structure of the force, the type of cases he got involved in, and his past role up in Manchester as a younger officer. Deep knew all about Operation Archangel, the recent operation to target sexual crimes on the London tube network, and he even referenced the case of Natalie Long's disappearance.

In return, Deep had talked through his pan-American Deep Distribution rail freight company in forensic detail, enthusing like an excited child about how it had grown from a relatively small start-up, to the biggest mover of freight across the United States. Cullen had mischievously considered asking his host about the events in the town of Hope, but had resisted and Deep hadn't offered anything up on that particular blot on the copy book.

There was no doubt that Deep was obsessed with everything train related, and it did certainly put his Deep Sleeper vanity project in context. Deep Sleeper's locomotive - Deep Sleeper One - was a renovated freight train, the first train that he had purchased for his distribution company.

Cullen emerged into the restaurant. There were still people eating at the tables, but Zack and Professor Brody had gone. More guests were now milling around the bar, sipping back brightly coloured cocktails.

'Detective Cullen!' someone said from his left. He turned, not intending to stop, but was held back by the man who tugged at his sleeve. 'You're the police detective, aren't you?' the man asked, holding a cocktail that was obviously not his first.

Cullen nodded and forced a smile.

The man lent in too close to Cullen's ear. The man's breath was fruity and alcoholic. 'Are you here undercover, Detective?'

Cullen stepped back, peeling the man's hand off his sleeve. 'It would appear not, given you know who I am.'

The man laughed. He raised a finger to touch Cullen's chest. 'Watch our host,' he said. 'Keep an eye on him.' He leant in again. 'He's ruthless. And I don't trust him. I don't even know why I'm here.'

Cullen pulled away slightly but wanted to keep the

conversation private. 'What do you mean, you don't know why you're here? I don't understand.'

'Neither do I!' the man laughed again. 'But maybe you can work it out, it's your job after all, isn't it, Detective? Solving the mystery. So go and solve it, my man!'

He slapped a hand on Cullen's back, before spinning around back towards the bar, leaving Cullen standing there, wondering.

~

THE INEBRIATED MAN'S words played on Cullen's mind as he returned to his cabin.

I don't even know why I'm here.

Cullen could have said the same about himself. He considered calling Zack, to talk through what the young journalist had wanted to tell him just before the boarding call had come through in London.

Maybe what he had to say would shed some light on all of this.

But it was gone eleven, and Zack might well be asleep. The conversation could wait until the morning. So, he penned a text message inviting Zack to meet him for breakfast at eight thirty. Hopefully he would pick it up in time, but if not, there would be chance to catch him later tomorrow morning before they arrived at Tulloch.

Within seconds a message pinged back.

Sounds good! See you then.

Satisfied with the morning arrangements, Cullen texted Sarah goodnight - once again, receiving an almost immediate reply - before readying himself for bed. He stood by the window, peering out at the pitch darkness for a few minutes, looking forward to the spectacular views that would come with the dawn.

Eventually, Cullen climbed into bed and flicked off the light at the wall. He shifted into the right position - the double bed was surprisingly comfortable, and did actually accommodate his six foot plus frame amply. Many a hotel room had failed in that respect over the years, resulting in a fitful night's sleep and aching limbs come the morning. The quality of the bed was just another indication of the careful design of Deep Sleeper.

The train was smoother than he had imagined, but the motion was of course still noticeable. The rolling and rocking did however seem to help, and Cullen was asleep in a matter of a few minutes.

Detective Cullen, thank you for joining me on board...

Cullen woke with a start, the words of Daniel Deep rising from his subconscious as sweat snaked along his brow. The room was unbelievably hot, and the sheets were sodden. He moved across to turn on the air conditioning at the wall. The time was just gone seven, and when he rolled the blinds up at the far side of the cabin, low morning sunlight blasted through.

Through still bleary eyes, Cullen admired the stunning views of the Scottish countryside for a few minutes. There was no chance he was going to get back to sleep, so he showered and dressed, before heading out to explore the train before he believed the rest of the passengers would emerge.

Cullen headed right, towards the rear of the train, passing through several passenger carriages before reaching the observation car. The car was designed with floor-to-ceiling windows that offered a panoramic view of the stunning Scottish landscape beyond. As he'd hoped, the car was devoid of people, so he settled into one of the comfortable armchairs and marvelled at the breathtaking view outside.

He felt like he could stay here for the rest of the journey, as the train snaked its way through the rugged Scottish countryside. They would be passing by mountains, deep valleys, and shimmering lochs, and surely there was no better vantage point - on the ground at least - than here.

Cullen was lost in the beauty of it all, when the interruption came.

'Detective Cullen.'

He turned to see Professor Brody standing over him.

22

Previously

DANIEL DEEP PROWLED around his luxurious San Fransisco office, with its views across the bay to the Golden Gate Bridge. He moved between the impressive collection of fitness equipment that he was able to utilise during the working day, kicking out angrily at the top of the range running machine as he passed it.

What a monumental waste of time!

He had just received the email confirming the results of his medical tests, following his emergency trip to the hospital and a subsequent visit to the high-end clinic in town where he had his full body scans. He still couldn't believe what he had been told and was now there on his screen, like a death knell.

Deep collapsed into his leather chair, head in his hands gripping his hair tightly, replayed the scene from forty-minutes ago, trying to process what had happened and willing things to turn out differently.

'Mr Deep, I'm afraid the results are not what we had hoped for," the doctor had said, his voice sympathetic but firm.

'What do you mean?' Deep had asked, trying to keep his voice steady.

'The scan showed a mass in your brain, which is malignant,' the doctor explained. 'I'm sorry to say that it's advanced and inoperable.'

'Inoperable?' Deep said, struggling with the concept. 'You're saying it's terminal? How long?'

The doctor, well versed in delivering sobering news, even to billionaires, hadn't missed a beat. 'I estimate you have around six months to live.'

Daniel felt his heart sink as he took in the doctor's words. Six months. That was all he had left?

'Is there anything we can do?' Daniel asked, desperation creeping into his voice.

'We can start you on a course of treatment to manage your symptoms and improve your quality of life,' the doctor had replied. 'But I'm afraid there is no cure for this. I'm very sorry, Mr Deep.'

Daniel had sat in stunned silence as the doctor continued to explain the treatment options available to him. He felt as if the ground had been ripped out from under him.

Deep opened his eyes, back in the present, and once again read the email confirmation from the clinic.

Brain tumour. Inoperable. Terminal.

Just like with his father.

He banged a fist down hard on the desk, causing the keyboard to jump.

He had always prided himself on his incredible health and fitness levels, and the thought of something as mundane as cancer taking him down was completely unacceptable.

'No,' he muttered to himself, slamming his fist onto his desk for a second time and then a third. 'This is not possible! Not acceptable!'

How the hell had they missed this before now?

He snatched up the desk phone.

'Dr Kochanski, where is he?'

'He just phoned through,' his personal assistant Emily said hesitantly. She had seen Daniel in the corridor, and was sure something bad was going down, but knew him well enough not to ask. 'He's stuck in traffic,' she explained. 'There's been an accident downtown, but he should be here in a few minutes.'

'He'd better be,' Deep growled. His personal physician was very good, and had been by his side for nearly ten years now, but like most people, he was replaceable. Slamming down the receiver, Deep began furiously typing out messages to his personal trainers, his chefs, and his wider medical team, demanding to know how this could have happened. He had spent millions on his health, on supplements, on experimental treatments, on anything that might give him an edge. And yet, it seemed that his wealth and power couldn't save him from the inevitable.

As he sat there, feeling the fear and anger boil inside him, a seductive thought began to creep into his mind. What if he didn't have to accept this diagnosis? What if he could use his wealth and influence to find a way to beat this thing? He could triumph where others would fail.

As he waited for Kochanski to arrive, he obsessed over the idea, pouring over potential solutions through a series of AI searches that took him on a wondrous tour of modern medicine.

He was lost in thoughts when there was a knock on the door.

'Come.'

Dr Kochanski entered, looking uncharacteristically flustered. He was red faced and sweaty, and had evidently been running. The exertion would do him good, as the sixty-two year old had been putting on some weight recently, Deep had noticed.

'I'm so sorry, Daniel,' he said. 'So very sorry.'

Instinctively, Deep assumed the doctor was apologising for his lateness, but he realised after a more careful examination of his expression that he was referring to the news of Deep's diagnosis.

'Sorry for what?' Deep replied brightly.

That threw him off balance. 'Sorry for...your news.'

Deep mustered a smile. 'I didn't call you here for sympathy. I called you here for solutions, Dr Kochanski. Please, do take a seat.'

The doctor did as requested, shifting in his chair as Daniel scanned another journal article on screen that he had found, offering what purported to be a miracle cure for brain cancer. It involved injecting bull's blood directly into the tumour.

'The clinic were not very helpful,' Deep said. 'They didn't offer me any treatment options. But I've found some promising ways forward. For example, this one.' He spun the screen around so that the doctor could see the bull's blood paper.

Dr Kochanski's eyes narrowed as he read the article, while Deep watched on.

'What do you think?' Deep asked.

'I'm...'

'There are other avenues,' Deep interjected, clicking through to another paper, this time involving cryotherapy whereby the brain's temperature would be lowered for several hours each day to arrest the growth of the mass. 'This one, and a few others, some really exciting, boundary-pushing treatments.'

Dr Kochanski's eyes slid away from the screen too quickly, and across to Deep.

'I'm so sorry, Daniel. I read the reports from the clinic, and have looked at the scans in detail. I'm afraid there is no way out of this.'

Deep shook his head.

'You haven't even given these papers a proper look,' he said to Kochanski, gesticulating towards the screen. 'Go home, study them with that sharp mind of yours, then come back to me with your recommendations. And we can take things from there.'

'I'm sorry, Daniel,' he repeated simply. 'None of these will work, because the situation is so grave. And also, these ideas, they are largely unproven, and maybe even harmful, even if there were treatment options. We...you...need to focus on how best to manage the situation, which of course, I am here to help with. And I know it will take time to comprehend what has happened, what is happening. But I'm there for you, every step of the way.'

'Leading me to my grave,' Deep added bitterly. 'Will you be there, to shovel on the soil? Is that all you have to offer?'

'Daniel,' Dr Kochanski tried to reach out, but Deep snatched his hand away. 'I'll be there for you. You don't have to do this alone.'

'Get out,' Deep replied softly.

'Please, Daniel.'

'I'll pay you what you're owed. Just go.'

'It doesn't have to be like this, and it's not about the...'

Deep kept his tone even, but the menace was there and growing. 'You've failed me. Now *get* out of my building, and my life, before I have to throw you out myself.'

Dr Kochanski gave a sad smile, but nodded and rose from his chair. He strode over to the door, but paused and turned before exiting. 'Daniel. You have my number, at any time, day or night, just call me. These coming months, you'll need support, you'll need people alongside you. Don't push everyone away; it will make things so much harder.'

Daniel Deep didn't reply, instead just turning his chair and himself around to face the window. A few seconds later he heard the sound of the office door closing.

He gazed up at the clear blue sky, tracking a passenger plane as it soared overhead.

The cancer was growing in mass, taking control, consuming him from the inside out. He could feel it now inside his skull, the lump squatting there in his brain like the most unwelcome house guest. There was no running away from this alien invader. He could flee to far away lands in one of his private jets; to the sun-drenched beaches of Rio, the towering mountains of Nepal, the ice fields of Antarctica, and it would still be there.

Inside him.

Tightening its death choke.

He pressed the intercom to call through to Emily. 'Cancel all my appointments for the next few days,' he instructed. 'I need some time to think.'

As he cut the call, the realisation setting in that he was truly going to die, Daniel Deep was consumed by a darkness unlike anything he had ever felt before.

Deep knew that his life was about to change in ways he couldn't even begin to imagine.

23

Present Day

'MIND IF I JOIN YOU?' the Professor asked. 'Or would you prefer the solitude?'

'Please, take a seat,' Cullen said, appreciating the right sort of company; after all, he had wanted to speak to the Professor anyway.

Professor Brody joined him on the chair opposite and gazed out of the window. Cullen watched him, musing on something, waiting for the questions that were obviously going to come.

'I had a good chat last night with your friend Zack,' Brody began. 'He's a very smart kid,' he added, smiling. 'Well, he's not exactly a kid, but he is to me, if you know what I mean.'

'Me too,' Cullen empathised. Zack was in his early twenties; Cullen was double his age, and felt like their relationship was a father-son thing, and Brody was probably twenty years older than Cullen.

'He told me that you're a detective chief inspector, with the British Transport Police,' Brody said.

'That is true.'

'And that Daniel Deep invited you on board to head up security.'

'That was the plan,' Cullen replied. He decided to trust the professor and tell him the full story, or at least as much of the story as he himself understood. 'But it also wasn't the plan.'

'I don't understand.'

'We were asked to provide security for the journey - well, my boss was asked that I accompany the train in my official transport police role. But it turns out that Deep already had that covered.'

'With his goons, you mean?'

Cullen nodded. 'Highly trained, best in the business goons, I think is the correct term,' he smiled mischievously.

'I had a run in with one of them last night,' Brody revealed. 'Tried to get to speak to Deep just after we first boarded - thought I'd get in there early, grab a few minutes with him before everyone else tried to get their piece.'

'What happened?'

'Some guy called Karl, built like a brick outhouse, told me that he wasn't taking private meetings.'

Cullen thought back to how last night Deep had not only invited him to a private meal, but had kept him there for hours. The billionaire was open to meetings, but just with the people of his choosing.

'I tried to push my luck, told Karl that it was urgent, and that Deep really needed to hear what I had to say, but there was no chance. I suspect Karl had been warned about me.'

'Warned?'

Brody smiled with some pride. 'I'm a trouble maker, for those who make trouble.'

'Tell me more.'

'I'm an environmental hazard specialist. Back in the States, I represent communities against those who have damaged them - big business and their owners. I had been supporting one community against Daniel Deep and his company, Deep Distribution.'

'The town of Hope,' Cullen said.

'Yes, that's right. You know about it?'

'Zack told me about what happened. Part of my background checks on Deep.'

Brody nodded.

'You said you *had* been supporting the community,' Cullen picked up.

'Yes,' Brody said, 'well spotted.' He chewed over his words. 'I can trust you, Detective, can't I? I mean, you're not working with Deep, are you?'

Cullen wasn't offended by the question. 'You can trust me. And no, I'm definitely not working with Deep.'

Brody nodded, satisfied. 'I had been supporting the town of Hope, until Daniel Deep got an associate to blackmail the Mayor to drop the legal case.'

'You sure that happened?'

Brody leant in, lowering his voice, even though the carriage was still empty apart from the two of them. 'One hundred percent. You've done your background checks on the man - you must know he's a nasty piece of work. Ruthless. I've worked against some bad guys in my career - the full range - but no-one quite as sinister as Daniel Deep.'

Given what Cullen had already read and heard, Brody's character analysis was no surprise. But it did raise interesting questions about why Brody was on board Deep Sleeper.

This was becoming a compelling pattern and Cullen was never one to leave such a thing uninvestigated or, wherever possible, unexplained.

'I know this sounds like a stupid question,' Cullen said. 'Your work, supporting communities like Hope, you are paid, aren't you? It's a job?'

Brody laughed. 'Oh yes, I've got my bills to pay, just like everyone else.'

'But you're not being paid to be here, are you? Not if Deep scared off the people of Hope.'

'That is correct.'

'Then why are you here?'

Brody leant in again. 'Because I don't like the bad guys to win. I detest bullies. My childhood was a misery because of people like Daniel Deep, and I guess I don't want to let this go.'

'Even though the people of Hope don't need your support any more?'

'Hope *do* need my support,' Brody corrected. 'And they've still got it, for as long as it takes.' He eyed Cullen, full of determination, his bright eyes sparkling behind his wire framed glasses.

'What are you hoping to achieve?'

'I want to get the chance to talk to Deep face to face, convince him to do the right thing. I want him to set up some proper long term health monitoring in Hope, to clean up his mess properly, and make sure he invests more into his trains so that this never happens again.'

'You think he'll listen, even if you do get the chance to talk to him?'

'I did think that's why he invited me on the journey,' Brody said. 'When the call came through from his PA, I thought that's what it was all about - making some kind of offer on board this train, wiping the slate clean. Maybe it is about that. But judging by last night, then probably not,' Brody conceded. 'He might have invited me to try and undermine my independence, now I've taken his offer of hospitality. Still, it was an opportunity I decided I had to take, even if it backfires.'

'You really think Deep might have invited you to undermine your reputation?'

Brody nodded. 'There's every possibility. But it's not going to work with me; I won't be intimidated. So today I shall try again to talk to the guy, and if that fails, I'll try again, and again, until Daniel Deep, Karl the bodyguard, and the other cronies wish I'd never been invited on this trip.'

24

Present Day

Cullen arrived a little early for breakfast, hoping that he might catch sight of the man who had cornered him at the bar the previous night. He was surprised though when he did actually see him, sitting alone, breakfast already half-eaten.

Intrigued by his comments and the air of resignation that seemed to hang over the man, Cullen approached him cautiously. As he drew closer, he noticed the bags under the man's bloodshot eyes.

'Morning,' Cullen said, his hands against the opposite chair, not sitting down just yet.

The man, mouth full of food, looked up, weary-eyed and reddened with horror. Despite his intoxication the night before, he obviously remembered their encounter.

'I'm so sorry for last night,' he said at last, swallowing the mouthful of breakfast and grimacing. 'I'm really embarrassed. I shouldn't have grabbed you like that.' He shook his head at the memories.

'It's fine,' Cullen brushed off. 'Don't worry about it. I'm Paul.' He held out a hand.

The man grimaced again as he shook hands. 'Joseph; Joseph Hamilton.'

'Are you okay?' Cullen asked. He certainly didn't look okay, although Cullen obviously knew what the most likely explanation was.

'Couldn't sleep last night. Room was spinning and *so* hot. I could feel every rock and roll of the train. Just awful. I was hoping this breakfast would help,' said the man. 'But I think it might be making me feel worse.'

'Or just taking its time,' Cullen joked. 'Mind if I sit down for a second or two?'

After a moment's hesitation, no doubt not particularly wanting the company, Joseph gestured to the empty chairs across from him. 'Please, have a seat.'

Cullen settled into the chair. 'I'll only keep you for a moment.'

'Sure, no problem.'

Cullen noticed the waiter eyeing him from across the carriage. He was probably noting the fact that he was sitting at the wrong table.

'Last night, you said you didn't trust Daniel Deep, that he was ruthless. You also said I should keep an eye on him. Why?'

'Please,' Joseph said, 'I'd rather not…'

Cullen glanced up at the waiter, who was now busy folding some napkins. 'What's your relationship with Deep? How do you know him?'

A wistful smile touched Joseph's lips. 'I had the misfortune of going into a business deal with Daniel Deep,' he revealed.

'Go on...'

'There's not much to tell,' he said. 'I owned a tech company, AI, we were doing really well; one of the best star-tups in Silicon Valley. Had a fantastic, young team of harding working people. Then eight months' ago Daniel Deep reached out, we met and he offered to buy a controlling stake in the company with the promise that he'd help us grow while also allowing us to maintain our independence. I stupidly believed him, even though I'd heard stories of what he could be like. He destroyed everything I had worked so hard to build.'

'What happened?'

Joseph's gaze hardened, his voice tinged with a mix of anger and frustration. 'He took the company, broke it apart, absorbed our tech into his other businesses. Got rid of all the workers. Even me.'

'Can he just do that?'

'Daniel Deep can do pretty much whatever he wants,' Joseph replied. 'He's got plenty of influence in high places, and can get away with things that other people might not be able to. Power, money and ruthlessness - it's a formidable combination.'

'I can see why you feel the way you do,' Cullen said, about to ask the obvious question. 'But if I was you, the last place I'd want to be at the moment, or even again, is in the company of the man who ruined your life.'

Joseph nodded. 'You would think so, wouldn't you?' he said sadly.

'So why are you here?'

'Because I received the invite, and a small part of me

wondered whether Deep was holding out an olive branch. I thought that, maybe, he'd asked me here by way of an apology; possibly to offer me something, a new business opportunity.'

'You still think that?' It was a plausible assumption, although the more Cullen heard about Deep, the less likely it seemed he would be the kind of person who would ever apologise and offer an olive branch.

Joseph shrugged. 'Yesterday, before we boarded, I was still hopeful. Actually, I was quite excited - things have been so hard these past few months, I sunk into depression with it all, and I struggled to see a way out. So this felt like a turning point. But last night, I started to have doubts, and by the end of the evening I'd convinced myself that Deep invited me here as some kind of sick joke, to rub my nose in his success and hold a mirror up to my failure.'

'That was probably just the drink doing the thinking,' Cullen replied, wanting to lighten the man's mood.

'Possibly,' he shrugged. 'But I worry I've just walked into a trap.'

'That sounds dramatic.'

'It's just how I feel this morning.'

Cullen thought on something. 'Last night, you asked me to solve the mystery. Did you mean anything by that? Or was it just the drink?'

Joseph laughed. 'I can't remember saying that. Did I say that?' He was thinking about it, looking impressed with his drunken self. 'You know, this is a mystery. That's how I feel. It's all a damn mystery. Do you agree?'

'It certainly has those vibes,' Cullen agreed, as he spotted Zack entering the carriage.

25

Present Day

'ZACK, YOU LOOK REALLY TIRED.'

Cullen slid into the seat opposite Zack, as the young journalist stifled a yawn. He really did look awful.

'Hardly slept,' he replied, yawning again. He shook his head. 'It's a sleeper train, you should be able to sleep, that's in the name. Did you sleep okay?'

'Like a baby,' Cullen smiled, amused by Zack's reaction and half-asleep state. 'What was the problem, too hot? I woke up early, feeling like I was inside a sauna.'

Zack hesitated. 'No, not the heat. I...'

Cullen's interest was piqued. 'You can tell me...'

Zack put a hand to his head. 'It's really stupid, but...' He looked up at Cullen. 'I couldn't relax. As soon as I climbed into bed, my mind started racing, listening to the sounds of the train on the tracks, every jolt, every roll, worrying that the train was going to derail. It was like I had to stay awake, to make sure that the train stayed on the tracks, as if by concentrating on it, I could make sure we were okay.'

He yawned again.

'It's so stupid. And then when I did get to sleep, I had the worst dream. We were on board the train, heading for Dover, and it went careering over the cliffs, into the water.'

Cullen actually grimaced at the thought. 'I used to be the same with flying. Got into a situation where I'd spend the whole flight focussing on the sound of the engines, willing the plane to stay airborne. It was pretty awful.'

Zack shook his head again. 'It's never happened to me before. I'm dreading the night back now.'

'You need a distraction,' Cullen said. 'Listen to music, or watch some TV. If it means you stay up most of the night, don't worry. I expect you'll zone out eventually and fall asleep.'

Zack smiled. 'Are you qualified to offer such advice?'

Cullen smiled back. 'What do you think?'

'Anyway, Zack,' said, 'I need caffeine, and lots of it.'

A waiter filled their cups and took their food orders, while Cullen watched Zack trying not to yawn. He would have suggested that he tried to go back to bed, but they weren't far from their destination now and he knew Zack had work to do.

'So,' Cullen said, as they waited for their food. 'What were you going to tell me yesterday? Let me see if it's what I think it is.'

Zack was intrigued. 'You think you know?'

Cullen smiled. 'I think so.'

'Okay,' Zack said, looking a little sceptical. 'You want to go first with your theory?'

Cullen nodded. 'Happy to. My theory is that every guest on this train has had some kind of run in with Daniel Deep.'

Zack grinned, shaking his head but impressed. 'You're good,' he said, pointing a finger, 'you should maybe think of going into the police service or something. How did you reach that conclusion so quickly?'

'The guy over there,' Cullen indicated over to the table on the far side with a subtle eye movement, 'Deep bought his company and destroyed it, along with the guy's career.'

'Joseph Hamilton,' Zack said, not looking at all surprised at what Cullen had just said. After all, he had had the guest list in advance.

'He doesn't know why he's been invited aboard,' Cullen added. 'But he hoped it was because Deep felt sorry for what he had done to his company, and wanted to make amends.'

Zack raised a sceptical eyebrow at that.

'And Professor Brody,' Cullen continued, 'he's come up against Deep through the incident at Hope. Like Joseph, he also doesn't know why Deep has invited him along.'

'That's right. Very good. You've spoken with Professor Brody?'

'An hour ago - we bumped into each other in the observation car.'

'An hour ago?' Zack looked at his watch. 'You were up early.'

'Brody told me that he'd accepted Deep's invitation as he believed it was his best chance to get an audience with him, to try and persuade him to fund the clean up and health monitoring in Hope.'

'He said the same to me last night,' Zack confirmed.

'Did he tell you about his run in with the bodyguard?'

'Yes. Sounds like Deep doesn't particularly want to talk to him.'

'At least not last night,' Cullen said.

'But he did want to talk to you,' Zack noted, letting the comment hang in the air as he waited for a response.

'He did,' Cullen acknowledged.

'About your role?' Zack probed.

'I haven't got a role,' Cullen revealed.

'What?'

'Deep told me that he'd made up the story of wanting me to provide security, to get me on board.'

Zack was confused. 'But, why?'

'That's what I've been trying to work out,' Cullen replied. 'Deep said he knows about me because he's fanatical about trains...'

'Which is certainly true,' Zack interjected.

'Oh yes, that's definitely true. He quizzed me for two hours last night, about the subject. It was pretty intense, and quite tiresome by the end.'

'So he really is a fan?' Zack said, nodding. 'He wanted you on board the train because he's a fan of yours. You have a billionaire groupie.'

'Somehow I doubt that...'

They paused their conversation as the food arrived. A cooked Scottish breakfast for Cullen, and smashed Avocado on toast for Zack.

'That looks...green,' Cullen said, looking with some scepticism at Zack's plate.

'You should try it,' Zack enthused. 'Really nice.'

'Maybe another time,' Cullen replied, cutting into a juicy, looking like it was ready to burst, sausage.

'What's your theory?' Zack asked, in between chewing.

'For why Deep drew up a guest list full of people who have reason to dislike him?'

'I don't have one,' Cullen admitted. 'Not yet, anyway. I need more information, and more time to think.'

'Well you've not got long,' Zack replied. 'Just the rest of the weekend.'

'More than enough time,' Cullen joked. '*If* I get the right information. Tell me more about some of other passengers. Not like you did in the waiting room - tell me about their relationship to Deep. And why you didn't give me the full picture before.'

Zack nodded, reddening. 'I didn't deliberately keep it from you,' he said. 'I had the manifest, did some background checks on their bios, but the pieces didn't actually fall into place until yesterday. I'd known, yes, that some of them had come up against Deep in the past, but then I suddenly realised, they all had *something* similar in their backstory. All of them. I was going to tell you, remember, just before boarding, when we were interrupted?'

'Fair enough,' Cullen conceded, feeling a little mean for challenging Zack like that. But it had been an obvious question, and whether Cullen had a natural affinity with the young journalist or not, if he thought Zack had deliberately kept something like that from him, he wouldn't have been happy.

'I'll tell you all I know about them,' Zack continued. He then ran through, in hushed tones, the various backstories of Deep Sleeper's guests, and their relationship with Daniel Deep. The vast majority of them were business people who had been ruined by Deep's acquisition of their company, but there were exceptions.

'What about Deep's cousin? You said he was one of the guests,' Cullen said.

'Stephen Dormer,' Zack replied. 'Yes, he's Daniel Deep's cousin, and a former business partner. Fifteen years ago, they set up a tech company together, but it turned sour when Deep ousted him from the Board following a disagreement about the direction of the business. I read that they hadn't spoken since.'

'But now he's on the train.'

'Now he's on the train.'

'And the lady, the Senator. What's her history with Deep?'

'Hilary Lancaster,' Zack said. 'She's a very experienced member of the US Senate. Just a few years' ago people were talking about her as a likely presidential candidate for the Democrats, but she bombed in the early rounds, coming second to last. It was a massive shock, because she'd been so favoured, and apparently she took it hard.'

'And what's that got to do with Deep?' Cullen asked.

'In her role as Senator, Hilary is also the chair of the National Transportation Committee. She came up against Deep when he was trying to expand his rail freight company, and they blocked a takeover of his main competitor Amerail. Deep was furious and blamed Hilary.'

'So he sabotaged her campaign?'

'That's the strong suspicion. There were credible rumours that Deep used social media targeting to undermine her campaign, spreading malicious stories about her and her husband - various unsubstantiated claims: that they'd be suspected of child mistreatment of their daughter back in the 1970s; that their marriage was just of convenience and that they actually had other secret partners; that they were siphoning money off from the campaign fund. The rumours were flying around, and gained momentum at grassroots, taking on a life of their own.'

'Nasty stuff,' Cullen commented. 'Not surprising she didn't do well in the nominations. And yet, here she is, on board Deep Sleeper, just like the others.'

'Here she is,' Zack echoed. 'For whatever reason.'

'Yes,' Cullen mused.

Suddenly the train slowed, and Zack looked up from his breakfast. 'We must be approaching the bridge.'

'The Douglas Viaduct?' Cullen replied. He'd read about it in the brochure in the cabin. It was widely regarded as one of the most impressive viaducts in the world, with many thousands of tourists visiting the Douglas Valley every year to gaze up in wonder at the sheer scale and engineering feat of the nineteenth century stone structure.

Zack gazed out of the window, craning his neck to try and look as far down the track as he could. 'We're on the right side,' he said. 'Take a look, it's beautiful.'

Cullen pressed his head against the window, and as the train moved slowly forwards he could see the bridge curving off to the left as it spanned the valley ahead. 'Why so slow? So we can enjoy the view?'

'Fifty miles per hour speed limit,' Zack replied, as they crossed onto the bridge and they both marvelled at the spectacular landscape hundreds of metres below. The valley was golden with the early morning sun, which lit up a thin ribbon of water running underneath, either side of steep wooded slopes. 'The angle of the curve onto the bridge from both sides is such that trains need to keep to this speed on the approach and as they cross.'

'Or what?' Cullen asked, fairly certain he knew the answer to that question.

'Or else we'd been seeing that valley from much closer quarters than we are now.'

Cullen looked down, imagining the train and everyone on it plummeting off the tracks.

It would be a terrifying way to go.

'Just as well the driver knows the limits,' Cullen mused.

Zack stared down at the drop. 'One hundred percent.'

PART III

26

Present Day

CULLEN STEPPED off the train at Tulloch station, which consisted of nothing more than a couple of platforms and a small stationmaster's office. The station itself was surrounded by amazing countryside views, and as Cullen turned back to look at Deep Sleeper he was taken in by the picture postcard beauty of it all.

He followed the rest of the passengers out through a low level, picket fenced exit gate, and left to the waiting coach that would transfer them to Daniel Deep's residence, Laggan Castle, just fifteen minutes east of here. As they waited to board, the crisp air carried a hint of excitement, blending with the sweet fragrance of nearby blooming flowers that had been planted along the station entrance.

The sleek, black coach with heavily tinted windows growled to life, its engine rumbling, as the automatic door hissed open and a rather rotund man stepped off.

'Bags in the hold, if you please,' the man said, in a pleasant Scottish drawl. He pressed a button on the side of the vehicle and the panel along the side opened up.

Cullen swung his overnight case inside, while the others - many of whom had much larger amounts of luggage - followed suit. He helped Hilary Lancaster with her huge bag, receiving a hearty thank you and smile from the Senator.

Climbing on board the coach, he was greeted by its plush leather seats and cool air-conditioning. The other guests followed, finding their seats and settling in for the scenic journey ahead.

'May I?' Cullen heard, as he gazed out of the window.

It was Hilary Lancaster, standing over him and gesturing at the empty adjacent seat.

'Of course,' Cullen said. 'Be my guest.'

Hilary slid gracefully into the seat and smoothed down her floral skirt. 'Well, let's see what the next day or so brings,' she said. 'I'm Hilary', she said, offering her hand.

'Paul,' Cullen said. 'Paul Cullen. Pleased to meet you.'

'Ah, the police officer?'

Cullen had to laugh. 'Is there anybody who doesn't know?'

Hilary smiled. 'We're all relying on you, Inspector Cullen, to protect us. The good old fashioned British detective.'

'Protect you? From what?'

Hilary chuckled. 'From our host, of course! He's a dangerous man.'

'So I've heard. But are you serious, about needing protection?'

'Good morning ladies and gentlemen,' a jocular voice cut across on the coach's speaker system. 'My name's Donald Argyll, and I'm your chauffeur to and from the station, today and tomorrow. As we make our way to Loch Laggan, I will do my very best to point out the many natural wonders we have around these parts. As you might have guessed, I won't be humble when it comes to talking about the beauty of the place I am so fortunate to call home.'

The coach began to roll forward, gliding smoothly along the winding road that led away from the train station. The windows were large and offered expansive views of the picturesque countryside. Lush wooded slopes came down right towards the road as golden sunlight dancing through the leaves of the trees.

Cullen listened intently as their knowledgeable guide, with his warm, Scottish lilt began to paint a vivid picture of the local area and its rich history.

'Welcome, ladies and gentlemen, to the stunning Scottish Highlands,' the guide began, their words carrying a contagious enthusiasm. 'As we make our way to Mr Deep's castle, I'll be your guide, sharing tales of the land we traverse.'

As the coach meandered along the road, the guide's voice weaved captivating stories, recounting legends of long-gone clans, heroic battles fought on these very hills, and the mystical folklore that permeated the air. Their words conjured vivid images in the minds of the passengers, transporting them to a bygone era where magic and mystery still lingered.

The guide pointed out landmarks along the way, each with its own tale of triumph or tragedy. He spoke of ancient ruins nestled among rolling hills, whispering of the ghosts that supposedly haunted them, and described the sparkling lochs that mirrored the sky, reflecting the tranquil beauty of the surrounding landscape.

The coach followed a winding path, climbing higher into

the emerald-covered mountains. As they ascended, the scenery grew increasingly breathtaking. Towering peaks kissed the sky, their rugged slopes adorned with cascading waterfalls and patches of colourful wildflowers. The air grew crisper, carrying with it the scent of pine needles and the promise of adventure.

Cullen could see how the passengers were captivated by the guide's storytelling, leaning forward, their eyes bright with anticipation, their hearts stirred by the grandeur of their surroundings. For a few minutes at least, the guests appeared just like all the other tourists.

As the coach rounded a final bend, the guide's voice grew hushed, filled with reverence. 'Ladies and gentlemen, feast your eyes upon Loch Laggan,' they announced.

'Wow,' Hilary remarked, 'now that is spectacular.'

Through the coach windows, a breathtaking sight indeed unfolded. Loch Laggan stretched out before them, its tranquil waters shimmering under the golden rays of the mid-morning sun. The imposing and impressive castle, constructed with dark grey stone, perched majestically on its shores, standing as a testament to the grandeur of its surroundings.

'Loch Laggan is a serene body of water that stretches out for miles. Its crystal clear waters are so still that the surface often looks like a perfect mirror, reflecting the stunning landscape of towering mountains and verdant pine forests that surround it,' the driver said. 'I'm sure you'll agree it looks beautiful now, but wait until this evening. As the sun sets, the sky is painted with hues of pink, orange, and gold, which casts the most amazing warm glow over the loch and the surrounding landscape. Standing on the castle's ramparts, the view is breathtaking. The loch stretches out before you, shimmering in the sunlight. In the distance, the mountains rise and fall like waves, and the forests stretch out as far as the eye can see. Am I selling this to you, folks?'

There was a murmuring of agreement.

The driver continued. 'The loch is home to a variety of wildlife, including trout and pike that swim in its depths, ospreys and golden eagles that soar overhead, and otters that can often be spotted playing along the shoreline.'

The driver's words tapered off, leaving a hushed silence in their wake, allowing the passengers to absorb the beauty that lay before them.

'You have to hand it to Daniel Deep,' Hilary said. 'He can certainly choose a nice place to live.'

'He certainly can,' Cullen agreed. It was no wonder that Daniel Deep chose this location for his Scottish home - a place of peace and tranquility, a true escape from the modern world.

'Outside, the castle has beautifully manicured gardens and grounds,' the driver continued, 'with paths leading down to the loch where you can take a boat out for a leisurely paddle. There's also a helipad for guests who prefer to arrive by air. As you approach the castle, you'll see that it's surrounded by a moat that's fed by the loch, adding an extra layer of protection to the already formidable structure. The drawbridge is made of sturdy wood and is pulled up at night to keep out unwanted visitors.'

The coach crunched to a stop on the gravel at the castle's grand entrance.

'I'm sure you'll have an experience you'll never forget,' the driver said, removing his seatbelt and opening the external door.

Cullen and his fellow passengers disembarked and

retrieved their luggage. The air was crisp and fresh, tinged with the scent of pine and heather.

'Savour every moment,' the driver added, by way of a goodbye, as he boarded the vehicle and swung out and away back around the Loch.

As the guests milled around the entrance, watching the departing coach, a helicopter appeared above, flying low across the Loch before disappearing around the back of the castle.

'Our host always likes to make an entrance,' a bitter voice said behind him. It was Joseph Hamilton. 'He could have travelled with us on the coach. But then again, why would he?'

Joseph moved off before waiting for an answer.

27

Present Day

'WELCOME TO LAGGAN CASTLE,' Emily Parker said, emerging from the entrance to the building and crossing the drawbridge. She must have arrived with Deep by helicopter. 'If you would just follow me please.'

Cullen and the rest of the guests crossed over the moat and through the main entrance. As they entered the grand double doors of Daniel Deep's castle home, they were immediately transported to a different era. The interior was a mix of old-world charm and modern luxury, with rich wooden paneling on the walls and intricate, ornate details on the ceilings. The floors were made of gleaming marble tiles, with plush carpets and tartan rugs adding warmth and texture to the space.

The foyer was grand and spacious, with a sweeping staircase leading up to the upper levels of the castle. The walls were adorned with a collection of antique weapons and artwork that depicted scenes from Scottish history, while the centrepiece of the room was a grand chandelier made of shimmering crystal. The air was perfumed with the scent of fresh flowers, which were arranged in vases throughout the room.

As the guests looked around, Zack joined Cullen at his shoulder. 'Impressive place,' he noted.

'Indeed,' Cullen agreed.

'Once you check into your rooms, feel free to explore the building,' Emily continued. 'The main hall is off to your left. You'll find it is a grand and impressive space, with a large fireplace and comfortable armchairs where you can relax and enjoy the warmth of the flames. The room is filled with the most beautiful antique furniture and artwork that has all been hand-picked by Daniel.'

'Where is Deep?' Joseph asked, scorn barely veiled in his tone.

'Mr Deep is currently resting,' Emily said, blinking at Joseph's impoliteness, 'and then has some important business to attend to, but he asks that you join him for this evening's reception as his special guests.'

'So he can't be bothered to be with us,' Joseph muttered, possibly just low enough in volume to evade Emily's ears.

But the other guests had heard, and Cullen felt the atmosphere thicken among them. Professor Brody was scratching at his beard, deep in thought, while Hilary Lancaster was shaking her head. Several other guests looked crestfallen.

'I'm sure we can entertain ourselves for the rest of the day,' Zack said, trying to inject some positivity. 'There are quite a few things planned for this afternoon, aren't there, Emily?'

Cullen glanced at Zack. He knew more about the agenda than he'd revealed, which did irk somewhat. Cullen wanted to be in the know, particularly in situations such as this, and he was surprised that Zack hadn't opened up more.

Maybe Zack knows more about Deep's intentions than he was letting on.

Cullen mused on that, while Emily nodded in response to Zack's statement.

'Yes, we've got an exciting agenda for this afternoon,' she confirmed. 'We've got a trip out on the Loch, in one of Daniel's private boats. And when we return, Daniel has arranged for a special performance of Macbeth in the great hall, which will then lead into dinner.'

'The Scottish Play,' Cullen mouthed to himself, thinking back to his school days of studying Shakespeare. Macbeth, one of his tragedies, had been their exam text. Cullen had never been the most enthusiastic of students from an academic perspective, but he did enjoy english literature and had a particular liking for Macbeth with its tale of lust for power and the subsequent loss that derived from its pursuit.'

'Sounds good,' Prof Brody commented. 'Who's performing it? A local amateur dramatics group? We did the same last year in our town.'

'The Royal Shakespeare Company,' Emily replied. 'They're currently performing in Glasgow as part of their award-winning tour, and have kindly agreed to come up today for this very special private performance.'

'Money talks,' Joseph muttered.

'Daniel is an extremely generous benefactor of the arts

across the United Kingdom,' Emily added, with a bright smile. 'You may have heard that last year he set up a multi-million pound fund for local theatres, to prevent their closure.'

'So we can go to our rooms now?' Stephen Dormer asked. Cullen hadn't realised he was on the coach too - evidentially Deep's cousin hadn't made the cut for the helicopter. 'Would be great to settle in for a bit before we go out on the lake.'

'Of course,' Emily replied. 'I also meant to say, the castle boasts a state-of-the-art gym, equipped with the latest machines. There is also a spa, which offers a range of treatments and therapies to help guests relax and rejuvenate. As Daniel's special guests, you are of course free to use any of these facilities at any point during your stay. Are there any other questions, before I grab your keys?'

'Why us?' a voice piped up. It was Hilary Lancaster. 'Out of everyone Daniel could have invited, why us?'

Emily nodded, as if she was expecting the question. 'I know some of you might have questions about why you were invited here for this very special weekend. All will become clear later at dinner, but for now, I'd like to pass on Daniel's heartfelt thanks for accepting the invitation to join him this weekend for Deep Sleeper's maiden voyage.'

The group looked from one to another, left to wonder for a little longer why out of all the people Daniel Deep knew, they were the ones standing here. Cullen was still thinking about that too, trying to piece things together, but there wasn't any more to go on since he and Zack had spoken at breakfast. And even though they'd been promised answers that evening, Cullen intended to find out some more himself before that point; call it police pride, or his personal drive to seek out the truth, he wasn't prepared to wait for Deep to reveal his intentions, if at all possible.

'So,' Emily continued breezily, 'if you don't have any further questions, let me just grab your keys and you can make yourself comfortable.'

28

Previously

EMILY PARKER PULLED up outside Daniel Deep's property, wheels crunching on the pure white gravel as her Fiat came to a stop. She sat there for a minute, marvelling at the irresistible views across towards the bay, fantasising what it would be like to call this place her home, and Daniel her husband.

She pulled down the overhead flap and gazed into the mirror, scrutinising herself. Emily was a striking woman, with a natural, effortless beauty. Standing at an average height, her slim build was maintained without overdoing the exercise.

Given the high profile nature of her role as Daniel Deep's personal assistant, she only wore designer clothes and high heels to work, but today she had gone for casual pretty, sporting a floral patterned dress that showed off her legs and shoulders, and a pair of white trainers.

Maybe Daniel would be pleasantly surprised by the difference.

Why had he invited her here, for the first time in all her years of employment?

And outside of working hours?

Emily took another moment to consider where she was in life. She'd grown up in a small town in the Midwest and worked hard to earn a scholarship to Harvard, being the first person in her working class family to enter higher education. She'd excelled in her studies and landed an internship at Deep Distribution during her final year of college. Impressed by her work ethic and intelligence, Daniel Deep offered her a permanent position as his personal assistant after she graduated.

She enjoyed working for Daniel, who had always treated her well. The job suited Emily, who was extremely organised and efficient, with a natural talent for managing complex schedules and handling high-pressure situations. He appreciated her strong communication and problem-solving abilities and had raised her salary several times in the three years that she had been working for him.

But there were downsides. Emily had always been a perfectionist, and this led to her working long hours and neglecting her personal life. She would go to great lengths to ensure that Daniel was satisfied with her work.

She knew what people said about him. And she had seen herself how he treated some of his staff. But she knew what he was really like, behind that hard facade. She had sometimes, albeit briefly, glimpsed the real Daniel Deep, or at least the person who he could be; the person she could help him to be.

'I really care for you, Daniel,' she said into the overhead mirror. 'I love you.'

Yes, her fierce loyalty to her boss was not just professional.

She could help him, she was sure of it. If only he would let her in.

But was he interested?

He'd never propositioned her. But then again, she hadn't seen him with anyone else either. For a time, she wondered if he might be gay, but she was pretty sure that it wasn't the case. More likely, she decided, was that it was a hidden vulnerability that saw him failing to reach out emotionally. She suspected that something had happened during his childhood, something traumatic, with that past shaping his present and future.

Although he'd never opened up about his personal life.

Just as he was presently hiding something important; the visit from the doctor, the descent into a darker mood, it signalled something bad.

Maybe he was going to open up now.

Finally, she exited the vehicle, feeling nervous and excited.

29

Present Day

CULLEN TURNED the key in the lock and entered the bedroom. It was spacious and luxurious, with a four-poster canopied bed, plush bedding and carpet, a huge flat screen television on the wall and a large desk with coffee machine and minibar.

He stuck his head around the bathroom door, and was surprised at how large the ensuite was - complete with a deep roll-top bathtub and separate walk-in shower. Everything in there exuded quality, with gleaming gold faucets, marble walls and a large ornate mirror.

Cullen dropped his bag on top of the luggage holder, and strode over towards the window, pulling back the heavy, sumptuous curtains. He had a breathtaking view of the Loch, which was gleaming in the sunshine just as spectacularly as the driver had described. Off to the right Cullen could see the boat that was their likely ride - it looked like a miniature super yacht you would see in Cannes; its aerodynamic, mirrored body seeming out of place in this remote part of the Highlands.

Part of him wished he could get out of the trip on the Loch, but it would be a good opportunity to find out more about the fellow guests.

He called Sarah, letting her know he'd arrived, and finding out how she was. She was intending to spend the day finalising plans for Philip's funeral, and Cullen once again felt a stab of guilt that he wasn't there in person to support her with that sad but important job. At least he had been effective at reaching Philip's friends with the news of the service, as the impressive confirmed guest list testified.

After the call, Cullen set off to explore the castle. He discovered an expansive and elegant living room, which provided stunning views of the Scottish countryside. The walls were lined with bookshelves, filled with leather-bound volumes which he leafed through. The furnishings were plush and comfortable, with deep sofas and armchairs upholstered in rich fabrics and the room was lit by soft, warm lighting.

The dining room was equally grand, with a long, polished wooden table that could easily seat the twenty guests. The room was already decorated with exquisite china, silverware, and crystal glasses, and the walls were adorned with oil paintings of Scottish landscapes. The chairs looked like something from a royal palace, with ornate carvings on the legs and backs.

This was one hell of a holiday home.

The group spent the afternoon on the Loch, on board Deep Venturer, Daniel Deep's vessel. Cullen chatted politely to the guests, including those he hadn't had the chance to speak to before now. They mingled on the deck, sipping champagne, and admiring the views of the Loch and its surrounds as the yacht sliced sedately through the still waters.

It was a truly magical place.

'Detective,' Hillary said, approaching, as Cullen watched a red kite circling overhead. 'Not a bad way to spend an afternoon.'

'I can think of worse places to be,' Cullen noted, although he could also think of better places - by Sarah's side being the main one.

'Look, what I said about us needing protection from Daniel Deep,' Hilary said, 'I was probably being a bit strong; I hope you didn't take me too seriously?'

'I always take those kind of things seriously,' Cullen replied, surprised by Hillary's change of heart.

She grimaced. 'Look, Daniel Deep is not the world's nicest individual - far from it. In fact, he's quite loathsome,' she chuckled. 'But,' she said, holding up a finger for emphasis, 'I don't believe he's dangerous; not in that way. His danger lies in the way he does business. He's a ruthless businessman and there's no doubt he's damaged a lot of people, but I'm not fearful of him on a personal level. I just wanted to clarify that. If I did think he was dangerous, I wouldn't be here, believe me.'

'Why *are* you here?' Cullen asked. 'That's what I still don't understand. Why are any of these people here?'

'I really don't know why he invited me,' she admitted. 'I guess we'll find out more this evening.'

'No, what I meant, is why did you accept?'

The Senator smiled. 'I very nearly said no,' she revealed, making absentminded circular motions along the rim of her champagne glass. 'But there was a part of me that was intrigued by the invite, and in the end I felt compelled to be here. You see, Detective, Daniel Deep is a very powerful man, and such power does often prove irresistible.'

'It still surprises me,' Cullen admitted.

Hillary laughed. 'Is it not the same with you, Detective? You chose to be here.'

'As part of my job,' Cullen countered politely. He liked Hilary, and didn't want to appear defensive.

'You didn't have a choice as to whether to accept the invitation?'

Cullen went to speak, but paused, eliciting a knowing smile from Hilary.

'I'm sure you were just as intrigued as the rest of us,' she said.

'Maybe you're right,' Cullen conceded. 'But if Deep had done the dirty on me in the past, I'd like to think I wouldn't be standing here right now.'

'Maybe,' Hillary said. 'But maybe not,' she added mischievously.

30

Present Day

THE TWO HOUR long performance of Macbeth was a triumph, taking place in an intimate theatre room that had been created in one of the old halls of the castle. Cullen had to admit he'd enjoyed it immensely, and for a time had been taken out of his thoughts of both Sarah and Philip, and of the mystery surrounding the Deep Sleeper trip.

'I'm sure you'll join with me,' Emily said, 'in congratulating the wonderful actors on such an amazing performance!'

The guests, including Cullen, clapped enthusiastically. He'd been surprised that Daniel Deep hadn't appeared to watch the play, but maybe he was still attending to the important business that Emily had referred to earlier.

Annoyingly, Cullen hadn't got any further in his thoughts about why Deep had brought these people together, so he would have to wait for the revelation at dinner.

'If you'll just follow me through to the dining room,' Emily said.

They followed, and were seated around the impressive table that Cullen had observed earlier that afternoon. Cullen was placed in between Zack and Hilary, with Joseph and Prof Brody across from him.

'Daniel will be along shortly,' Emily announced.

The anticipation was palpable in the few minutes before Daniel Deep entered. Their billionaire host strode in confidently and with purpose, dressed in a crisp, white open-collar shirt and dark skinny trousers. He reached the head of the table, and toyed with one of his gold cufflinks as he cleared his throat.

There was no sign of his bodyguards.

'Ladies and gentleman,' he smiled, eyeing everyone seated at the table as he remained standing. 'Welcome to my humble abode! I trust you enjoyed the train journey up from London on Deep Sleeper One, and the trip on the Loch this afternoon. I heard Macbeth was suitably amazing; sorry that I couldn't make it. Hilary, Stephen, Professor Brody, and all my very welcome guests, I know you are wondering what this is all about.' He placed his hands flat on the table. 'It's really quite simple,' he said, sounding serious all of a sudden. 'I've invited you here by way of an apology.'

Deep let that hang in the air, but none of the guests uttered a word.

'I want to apologise,' Deep continued, 'to say sorry to you all, personally, for how my actions over the past few years have affected you.' Deep made eye contact with each and every person, apart from Cullen and Zack. 'As you all know, I am a very successful businessman. I have achieved great things, and am one of the richest and most influential people in the world. However, recently I have reflected on some of my behaviour, which I have come to the conclusion was inappropriate. So, I invited you all here, as representatives of all those who I may have wronged, to say sorry.'

Cullen's eyes swept the table for a reaction. Most of the guests looked stunned.

Most of the guests...

'Is that it?' Joseph said.

Deep tipped his head towards him. 'Sorry?'

'I said, is that it? Sorry, but that's all?'

Deep smiled tightly. 'Well...'

'I mean, you destroyed my business, my whole life,' Joseph continued, increasing in volume. 'Because of you I have pretty much nothing, and you offer me a sorry, I feel bad. Sorry just doesn't cut it with me, Deep.'

Daniel Deep went to respond, but stopped himself for a few seconds of reflection. 'Joseph, let's meet afterwards about all this, talk things through.'

Joseph laughed bitterly. 'Oh, so you're willing to meet with me now? I mean, you weren't so willing when I tried to contact you all those times, were you? I'm sorry, but unless you're offering *me* genuine recompense for the damage you did, then you can shove your sorry up your ass.'

Cullen could see that Joseph was shaking, his hands gripping the table for support like he was on a white-knuckle ride. Deep would surely also see the highly charged state of the guy, and hopefully react accordingly.

'Let's talk, Joseph,' Deep said in a voice designed to sooth. 'I promise we'll get the two of us together.' He looked away from the man. 'And that goes for all of you,' he added. 'But for now, let's just enjoy the evening and the wonderful food we have to come.'

He clapped twice in quick succession and almost immediately a team of waiting staff appeared with the starter of seared hand-dived orkney scallops or a vegan option of pistachio parfait.

The main meal of fillet of Scotch beef was amazing and the desert of bitter chocolate torte divine. Cullen was enjoying the sweet treat so much that he hadn't noticed that Deep had left the table.

Not only that, but so too had Joseph Hamilton.

31

Present Day

Daniel Deep bent over the sink and splashed cold water onto his face, gazing at his dripping reflection in the mirror. He smiled at himself, still admiring the view as beads of water snaked along his sculptured jawline.

You just couldn't tell.

His mood darkened as he thought about the reality of his situation; but this wasn't the time to surrender. After all, he was heading to a victory of sorts, and to achieve that he needed to maintain focus.

Particularly with Cullen around.

He thought of the detective and their wide-ranging conversation on board Deep Sleeper One. Cullen hadn't been a disappointment and Deep certainly didn't regret inviting him along, but as he had always expected, he would need to be careful as Cullen was sharp, with his wits about him.

Deep had been watching the officer during the meal, and

you could see his mind ticking; Cullen sensed that something was amiss.

Cullen's suspicions just added to the excitement. If Cullen reached the answer too quickly, it was ruin everything, but Deep very much doubted that would happen.

Deep smiled broadly in the mirror, the darkness and doubt banished again.

He made to turn away from the sink just as the door to the washroom opened.

'Joseph,' Deep said calmly at the reflection in the mirror. He turned to face him, as Joseph let the door close behind him.

'What you said back there,' Joseph slurred, taking a faltering step towards him, 'about being sorry for what you've done, to me, all of us. I don't believe a word of it.'

'Joseph, you're drunk,' Deep replied, observing the man with quiet distain. 'I think you'd better go upstairs and sleep it off. We can talk about this another time.'

'I'm not drunk!' Joseph protested, 'and there's no time like the presents...present. We can speak now.'

'I was watching you, Joseph,' Deep replied, remaining in his position by the sink and his tone measured. 'During the meal. You've drunk a lot of wine, and I mean *a lot*. Which is fine, I mean, we're well stocked, but I think you've overdone it, my friend; you're unsteady on your feet, and your eyes are blood red.'

'I want proper recompense!' Joseph spat, actually sending visible lines of spittle in Deep's direction. 'I want *you* to recompense me for everything you've done.' He jabbed an accusing finger, lurching forwards. 'You've ruined my life!'

Deep shook his head. 'You've got to move on with your

life, Joseph. I've said my piece, and I hope it provides some sort of closure for you, I really do.'

'I'll show you closure!' Joseph shouted, bringing out a six inch butchers' knife from the inside of his jacket. The blade glinted under the bright lighting of the bathroom. He held it towards Deep with a shaking hand.

'Now Joseph, don't do anything stupid,' Deep said, sliding a hand into his trouser pocket and pressing the button. He then held up both hands and mustered a smile. 'Please, put down the knife.'

Joseph shook his head. 'Not going to happen.' He stepped towards Deep.

'Stay back!' Deep commanded, with his back pressed against the sink and nowhere to go. He glanced longingly towards the external door as Joseph took another step closer.

'You'll listen to me now, Deep.'

Suddenly the external door was kicked open and Karl, Deep's bodyguard, flew through it, hitting Joseph in the back of the ribs with laser-like accuracy before he'd even had chance to turn around and see what was happening.

Joseph cried out, folding at the waist and dropping the knife. Karl wrapped his arms around the back of Joseph's shoulders, pulling him up into a full nelson, stretching his body backwards.

'Please,' Joseph cried, grimacing as Karl increased the pull backwards, 'please, I wouldn't have used the knife, I wouldn't have actually used it, I wouldn't.'

Deep relaxed, straightening up against the sink as he observed Joseph struggle like a landed fish.

He bent down in one smooth movement and picked up the knife, holding the blade towards the floor.

Joseph's eyes widened in fear, and he tried, unsuccessfully, to break free from from Karl's vice-like grip.

'I'm not going to hurt you,' Deep said.

Tears were running down Joseph's cheeks. 'Thank you.'

Deep placed the knife on the sink behind him, before taking a step towards Joseph.

'I should call the police,' Deep said. 'Or just inform the officer enjoying his dessert in the room down the hall; I'm sure he'd be all too happy to arrest you for attempted murder, or whatever it was you were planning to do to me.'

'I'm sorry,' Joseph said, really crying now. 'I don't want to go to jail. My family, they'll have nothing.'

Deep ran his tongue around the inside of his mouth, musing on that. 'I'll tell you what, Joseph,' he said, finally, moving a little closer to the cowering man; he could really smell the wine on his hot breath. 'Let's not let this go any further.' He nodded at Karl to release his hold, and as the bodyguard did as commanded Joseph's body reformed into its natural position.

Joseph stared back in disbelief, holding a painful arm. 'Really?'

'You go upstairs, get an early night, and we can start again in the morning. We can forget all about what just happened here. There won't be any need to inform the authorities.'

'I don't understand.'

Deep shrugged. 'As I said during the meal, I've come to realise the error of my ways, and want to make things better.'

Joseph nodded, still looking bewildered.

'Right after the trip,' Deep continued, 'let's talk about really making things right for you and your family. I want to ensure that you are fully compensated for what I did to you.'

'Seriously?' Joseph was amazed but still not quite ready to believe what he was hearing. 'You mean financially?'

'I mean financially.'

Now Joseph did surrender to the good news. 'Oh, thank you, Mr Deep, thank you so much! Thank you!'

Deep tensed as he allowed a still-drunk Joseph to embrace him.

'Karl will help you upstairs to your room,' Deep said, pushing down his repulsion at this pitiful man as he peeled himself away from the guy. 'I'm sure the sleep will do you the world of good.'

~

CULLEN EXCUSED himself from the table and entered the foyer, just as he saw Daniel Deep, Karl and Joseph emerge from the toilets. It was strange, the three men coming out together, and it certainly piqued Cullen's interest.

'Is everything okay?' Cullen said, intercepting the men as they walked off in the opposite direction.

Deep turned around and smiled. 'Absolutely fine, Inspector,' he said. 'I bumped into Joseph in the washroom and we had a good chat about how I can make his life better. Didn't we, Joseph?'

Unconvinced, Cullen looked at Joseph for confirmation, who nodded enthusiastically. Cullen could see straight away from his gait and red eyes that the guy was drunk, but his reaction seemed genuine. Still, he wanted to make sure.

'Are you okay?'

'I'm fine,' he said, stepping back and forward as the alcohol continued to sluice around his body. 'I just need to get some rest in my room, and be ready for tomorrow. Everything is good now, Daniel and I have come to an agreement.'

Cullen looked at Deep.

'I just want to make things right,' he said.

'Good to hear,' Cullen replied, still surprised by Daniel Deep's public act of contrition, particularly given everything he had heard and read about the guy. But it was possible that people could change. Working in the force, dealing so often with the horrors that humans could inflict upon one another, it was easy to be cynical about the idea of rehabilitation and reconciliation. And yet, it did happen; there were examples from Cullen's own career where offenders he had helped to lock up had turned their backs on bad behaviour and gone on to live honourable lives.

Who was to say that the same hadn't happened to Daniel Deep?

But that kind of transformation often arose from a trigger of some kind; often through loss - of their liberty through a jail sentence, or the death of a loved one, for instance.

If Deep had changed for good, Cullen was interested in knowing what the trigger had been.

32

Previously

Twelve year old Paul Cullen wiped the sweat and rainwater off his forehead as he leaned against the rugby goalpost, catching his breath after a gruelling Friday evening practise on the outskirts of Wigan. The coach had just blown his whistle, to call time on the hour-long training session; the first of the season. Cullen had always loved training - almost as much as playing matches - but today's workout, in blustery, rainswept conditions, had been particularly intense and he felt like another few minutes and he might have been physically sick.

Thankfully, the whistle had come just in time.

As he watched his teammates pack up and head back to the changing rooms, he spotted a new face walking towards the field. The boy was tall and lanky, with a mop of curly brown hair and a friendly grin on his face.

'Hi there,' the boy said, extending his hand. 'I'm Philip. I just moved here from Manchester. Did I just miss the training? Thought it was at eight.'

'Seven,' Cullen corrected.

The boy looked disappointed.

'I'm Paul,' Cullen added, shaking Philip's hand. "Nice to meet you.'

'You too,' Philip replied. He turned around, watching the other lads traipse off towards the car park. 'I guess I'd better be going, then.'

'Fancy a kick about? I mean, while you're here. I've got my own ball, over there.'

'Fantastic!' Philip replied. 'I don't want to go back home yet; my little sister Sarah has some annoying friends round.'

Paul and Philip spent the next half an hour kicking and catching the ball, testing each other out with higher and higher "bombs", teasing grubber kicks along the floor, and dodging attempts at one boy to tag the other.

'You're good,' Paul said. 'You've played before.'

'For my old team in Manchester,' Philip confirmed, chipping and catching the ball. He spun it high into the air and caught it with ease.

'What position?' Paul asked, more impressed at this new arrival with each passing minute.

'Loose forward,' Philip said.

That figured, with his size and speed. 'Are you *really* twelve?' Paul asked.

Philip laughed. 'Absolutely!'

Over the next few weeks, Philip quickly became a valuable member of the team. He was fast on his feet and had an uncanny ability to read the game, making him a fierce competitor on the field. But it wasn't just his skills that drew

Paul to him - Philip had an infectious energy and a genuine kindness that made him an instant friend.

As they walked off the field together after another pounding practice, Philip turned to Paul with a mischievous grin.

'Hey, have you ever snuck into the swimming pool after hours?' he asked, gesturing towards the metal building off to their left. The small indoor, unmanned private pool was owned by the trade union social club, whose pitches the rugby team used for their practise and matches.

Paul raised an eyebrow. "Can't say that I have. Why?' He'd actually only been in there once, a few years ago for a birthday party of a classmate whose father helped to run the club. It had been lots of fun, and he'd often looked across to the building and longed for a second visit. But the pool was strictly off limits for public use.

'Well, I heard a rumour that there's a spare key hidden near the building,' Philip said. 'Underneath a rock on the edge of the field.'

'Really?'

Philip nodded, smiling. 'Once you're in there, no-one will know, and the pool will be ours for as long as we want! What d'ya say we check it out?'

Paul grinned back, feeling a rush of excitement. He had always been a bit of a rule-follower, but there was something about Philip's carefree attitude that made him want to live a little.

'Let's do it!' he said, pushing away his doubts and fears.

A few days later, as they slid back the doors to the building, kicked off their over-clothes and jumped excitedly into the warm waters of the pool, Paul knew that he had made a lifelong friend.

33

Present Day

Cullen woke early, at six am, the memories of a faintly disturbing dream already fading but still present.

He'd dreamt of the first time he had met Philip, at the rugby training ground. It marked the beginning of a decades-long friendship, which had remained strong throughout the various twists of turns of life - first the highs and lows of school and rugby, then relationships, careers, weddings, and most significantly, illness.

In the dream they'd been in the swimming pool, thrashing and splashing about, high as kites, laughing and joking.

And then something changed.

Philip had quietened, his expression blank, his body floating up to the surface of the warm water, until he was ramrod straight, looking up emotionless at the metallic ceiling.

Paul had waded his way towards him, calling out his name, but Philip didn't react. Instead he'd floated away, carried by a currant, and suddenly they were in colder, open waters, shrouded by a low hanging mist that kissed the top of the water and wrapped itself around the two boys.

Paul had watched in horror, powerless, as Philip drifted further and further away, out to the wide river mouth and the spooky sea beyond.

Turning back, Paul had swam for the shore, reaching the beach and stepping out across the sand.

Alone.

Cullen showered, thinking again about the dream. You didn't have to be a psychologist to interpret it. He had lost his friend, who had indeed drifted away from him; but taken by brain disease, not the tide.

He scrubbed at his body. Like in the dream, he had in effect just let it happen - Philip had been carried away from them, and he'd done nothing to help, once the dementia had really taken hold.

The guilt.

How do you deal with guilt when there's no longer any opportunity to atone for your actions?

He finished washing and stepped out of the shower, drying himself roughly. He'd tried to make amends for abandoning his friend; in recent times he had taken it upon himself to reconnect. And despite his fears, he'd enjoyed those times with Philip, taking him to the rugby, just being with him. Sarah had testified how much of a difference it had made.

But that only made him feel worse, now that Philip was gone.

If he'd made such a positive difference these past few months, how much more of a difference could he have made to his friend if he'd stuck with him from the very beginning?

His head still full of thoughts, Cullen decided to head out for a walk around the Loch before breakfast. Stepping out from the castle, the sound of birdsong filled the cool, crisp air and lifted Cullen's spirits. He headed off in a clockwise direction, around the Loch's shore. It was as he rounded the first rocky outcrop that he saw the person in the water.

Cullen paused, focusing on the individual, who was swimming front crawl out from the other side towards the centre of the Loch. He watched as they powered through the waters, without hardly a splash being made.

It was Daniel Deep.

Cullen watched in awe as Deep continued onwards. He thought back to what the billionaire had said about his love of wild swimming, and the health enhancing qualities he believed it brought. There was certainly no doubting Deep's commitment, at what was still an early hour in what must surely be bone-numbingly cold water.

But then something changed.

Cullen watched in growing concern as Daniel Deep's progress came to an abrupt halt, and he began thrashing about in the waters towards the centre of the Loch. Concern grew to horror as Cullen's heart pounded.

With Deep still struggling in the water, and no sign of his bodyguards or anyone else who could help, Cullen sprinted towards the shoreline. What he'd hoped would be a peaceful walk to clear his mind before the long day ahead, had turned into something very different.

Cullen kicked off his shoes and yanked his trousers down and off his legs. Also dispensing with his jumper, he entered the water, tensing at the colder than expected temperature as the water washed around his feet, then up to his waist.

So cold...

He started to swim, hauling his arms over the top of his head and kicking out with his legs to try and generate some momentum. But it was hard; the cold had shocked his body into near spasm, and within a few leaden strokes Cullen too was really struggling.

He gasped for breath and Loch water gushed into his mouth, like a dam breached.

Coughing violently, he tried to stand up and take stock, but the water was deep and he sank below the surface, feeling like he was being pulled down to the depths.

He thrust arms skyward, desperately clawing for something that wasn't there.

In the cold waters, fighting for breath, his thoughts turned again to Philip; the two carefree young boys, splashing in the warm pool, having the life of their lives.

One now dead.

The other dying.

Cullen sensed a shadow falling over him, and the water darkened.

Was this the end?

He wanted to call out Sarah and Amy's names, to somehow try and say goodbye from his watery grave.

And then, suddenly, he was moving upwards, the thrust taking him out of the water and into fresh air. He felt his body scrape along the side of something, and then come down on a solid surface.

'What the...' he tried to say, but instead launched into a fit of coughing as his body tried to eject the Loch water from his system.

'It's okay,' a gruff voice said, patting him on the back to encourage the murky liquid out. 'Get it out.'

Cullen opened his eyes and saw the sky. Two men were sitting over him, and he quickly realised that he was on a small inflatable boat, bobbing about with the combined weight of its occupants.

'We'll get you back to shore,' one of the men said, as the motor boat powered across the Loch.

'Deep,' Cullen managed to say, coughing again, trying to raise his head. His throat felt raw and scratched, all the way down, like he'd swallowed nails. 'He's in the water.'

'They're getting him now,' came the response. 'Don't you worry.'

They quickly reached the shore, and Cullen was helped off the boat by the two bodyguards. He was already feeling better, but was unsteady on his feet and shivering. They sat him down, wrapping a blanket around him, just as another inflatable came speeding towards them. Cullen saw the expression of the boat's pilot, and feared the worst.

Cullen watched anxiously as a man from the second boat stepped out, holding Deep's limp body in his arms.

The bodyguards on the shore rushed over to help and they carried Deep over to flat ground, lying him down gently on the grassy bank.

Together, they began performing CPR, trying to revive him.

Cullen wanted to help, but there was nothing more that could be done. So instead, he looked on and hoped for a positive outcome.

Finally, after what felt like an eternity, Deep coughed and sputtered, and his eyes fluttered open. Cullen breathed a sigh of relief.

'What happened?' Deep whispered, looking around in confusion and wonder like a baby just born to the world.

'We're not sure,' the man over him said. Only then did Cullen realise that the person who had just saved his life was his bodyguard, Karl. 'I think you had some kind of episode, in the middle of the Loch. One moment you were swimming, and the next, you went under the water.'

Deep tried to get up, but launched into a series of violent coughs which sent him back down towards the ground.

'I'd take it easy, Sir,' Karl advised, placing a steadying hand on his boss's shoulder.

Deep nodded reluctantly as the coughing subsided. Still obviously confused and disoriented, but improving already, he looked across and saw Paul Cullen; realising that he too was soaking wet.

'We need to get you both dry,' Karl announced. 'And something warm to drink.'

Cullen and Deep nodded their agreement as they gazed at each other, now bound by a shared experience.

For a second, Cullen thought that Deep mouthed something to him, but he was still struggling to focus and the moment was lost.

34

Previously

'EMILY, thank you so much for coming,' Daniel smiled, welcoming his personal assistant at the door. She was wearing a pretty dress, looking quite different from how she did at the office.

'My pleasure,' she smiled back, looping a curl of hair around her ear. Her blue eyes were bright, twinkling in the sunlight. 'This location, it's just amazing.'

'Thank you,' Deep replied.

'And the gardens,' Emily continued, looking around towards the front of the house, 'just stunning.'

'I have an excellent gardener,' he replied. 'Please, do come in and I'll show you around.'

She followed him through the lobby and into the living room, marvelling at the place and its views across towards the bay.

'It's even better than the photos,' she said, before pulling up short and blushing at the acknowledgement that she had obviously been looking online at his property - probably from the spread a couple of years ago in Time magazine where Deep had been interviewed at home about the rise (and dangers) of Artificial Intelligence.

'Things are usually better in the flesh,' he said breezily, in what was most likely his first ever attempt at flirting.

It seemed to hit the mark, judging by Emily's reaction.

'Drink?' Deep asked. 'I have a bottle of award winning wine that I've been saving for a special occasion.'

'Special occasion?'

The comment had certainly aroused her interest.

'Yes,' he said. 'Your first visit to my home, of course!' He moved across to the kitchen and opened the bottle, before handing her a glass and clinking a "cheers".

'This is lovely,' she commented, after taking a sip.

'Glad you like it.'

They walked across back to the living room and stepped through the already-opened huge bi-fold doors, onto the spacious balcony that overlooked the gardens and vista beyond.

'Wow,' Emily said simply.

'This is what money can buy,' Deep said dryly.

'Money, talent and imagination,' Emily corrected with a smile.

'You're too kind.'

'It's true,' she shrugged, wondering whether she was going too far. Her glass was already almost drained, and her head somehow already light from the mixture of alcohol, sunlight and powerful attraction she felt towards Daniel.

At work, it was easier to suppress, but here it was different.

They stood looking at the view, shoulders almost touching.

'There's something I want to tell you,' Deep said at last.

Emily turned to him, her face expectant and just inches away from his. 'Yes?'

I'm unwell...

I have terminal cancer...

I have an estimated six months to live...

I have something that you can help me with...

'I love you,' he said.

35

Present Day

INSIDE A PRIVATE STUDY at Laggan Castle, the air held a solemn weight as Paul Cullen and Daniel Deep sat across from each other. The room exuded an aura of grandeur, with towering bookshelves filled with ancient tomes and a fireplace crackling with warmth.

An hour since the dramatic events on the Loch, Cullen and Deep had washed and changed into dry clothes, with both men looking remarkably good for their experience.

'You asked to see me?' Cullen said, his sore throat now soothed from a couple of mugs of tea.

Daniel Deep nodded. He gestured at Karl, who was standing at the edge of the room, to leave them alone.

'You saw me in trouble,' Deep said. 'You saw me go under the water and jumped in to try and save me.'

'Try being the operative word,' Cullen said. 'I'm afraid I

overestimated my wild swimming abilities, or at least, underestimated how cold that Loch is. I certainly didn't get anywhere near you to be of any help.'

'Thank you,' Deep said. 'I really mean it. Thank you, for putting your life on the line.'

Cullen shrugged. He actually felt slightly embarrassed at his unsuccessful efforts to help, which had just drawn resources away from Deep's rescue.

'Why?' Deep said.

Cullen was confused.

'Why do it?' Deep added. 'Why risk your life like that?'

He looked genuinely mystified.

'Anyone in my position would have done the same,' Cullen lied. In fact, he knew from experience that it certainly wasn't always the case, or even the case in the majority of situations. As much as people would like to think that they would stand up and be the hero in a life-threatening event, often those present would be consumed by paralysis, with blind fear winning out over intentions of bravery.

Deep seemed actually troubled by Cullen's assertion; certainly lost for words.

'Your bodyguards saved you,' Cullen said. 'They're the real heroes here.'

'They're paid to save my skin,' Deep replied.

Cullen couldn't argue with that, although this morning's events were somewhat above and beyond the call of duty.

'Paid very well,' Deep added. 'But you, you risked your life for what? A stranger?'

'Not quite a stranger.'

'But if I had been a stranger, you would still have jumped in, wouldn't you?'

'Yes,' Cullen answer honestly.

Deep shook his head in what looked like disbelieving admiration, before his expression darkened.

'What if I were to tell you that you were wasting your time?' he said.

'I don't understand.'

'Trying to save me,' Deep said. 'You risked your life trying to save someone who can't be saved. You would, in effect, have died for nothing.'

'You're going to have to explain that one to me,' Cullen replied.

Deep nodded. 'Of course, of course.'

Paul's eyes searched Deep's face, noting a new weariness that clung to his gaze. It was as if the weight of the world suddenly rested upon the man's shoulders, a burden too heavy to bear alone.

'What is it?' Cullen asked.

'Inspector Cullen,' he began, hands steepled and his voice tinged with a never-before-heard vulnerability, 'there's something I want to tell you. I'm not even sure why. But here it is, something that very few other people know: I'm dying.'

Cullen leaned forward. 'Dying?'

Deep took a deep breath, gathering his thoughts before continuing. 'I have been diagnosed with a terminal brain tumour. It's inoperable. The doctors have given me only a short time left - a matter of months.'

'I'm really sorry to hear that,' Cullen replied, the weight of the revelation settling heavily upon him. He had never anticipated such an announcement or such a fragile vulnerability hidden beneath Deep's formidable exterior. The world suddenly seemed smaller, the lines between right and wrong blurred by the harsh reality of mortality.

'Me too,' Deep said. 'What happened on the Loch, it must

have been another seizure. I remember my head started pounding. It's happening more and more, like a thunder storm closing in. So I know I'm about to lose everything, have it ripped away from me, but I'm not going quietly.'

'It makes sense now,' Cullen thought out loud, finally understanding the motivations behind the trip. 'You wanting to make amends with people, before it's...'

'Too late,' Deep finished. His eyes glistened with unshed tears, a flicker of remorse crossing his face. 'It's my way of making amends, of finding some semblance of redemption. I wanted to mend the broken bridges, to bring everyone together before it's too late. The impending end has given me a newfound perspective, an understanding of the futility of holding grudges and nurturing hatred.'

Deep had parted the veil, allowing Cullen to see beyond the wealthy facade, beyond the controversies and the manipulations, and glimpse the humanity that lay beneath.

Maybe everyone could be saved.

At least those who wanted to be.

'I don't want to leave this world with regrets, Paul,' Deep continued, his voice trembling. 'I want to make amends for the pain I've caused and the lives I've disrupted. Deep Sleeper is not just a train; it's a journey of reconciliation and closure.'

Cullen witnessed the raw vulnerability in Deep's confession. Through Philip's illness and death, Cullen understood the weight of regrets and the yearning for redemption. In that moment, their roles as detective and billionaire blurred, replaced by two individuals united by the fragility of life.

'I believe in second chances, Daniel,' Cullen said, his voice filled with empathy.

A flicker of relief passed over Deep's face, as if a burden

had been partially lifted. The room felt suffused with a newfound sense of purpose and compassion.

But the individual listening just outside the door didn't believe a word of it.

36

Present Day

THE REST of the morning was a relaxed affair, with guests free to explore the castle and its surrounds some more. Cullen retreated back to his room for some rest and recuperation, exiting only to join the party for lunch.

'Up to anything interesting this morning?' Hillary asked Cullen, as they tucked into their food.

'Not much,' Cullen lied. He was impressed and not a little surprised that the dramatic events on the Loch seemed to have gone completely unnoticed by the rest of the guests.

It had all happened very early in the day, but Cullen had wondered whether someone had caught the action from one of the many bedroom windows overlooking the Loch.

'Disappointed that Mr Deep isn't with us,' Hillary noted, prompting a nod from the other guests, including a brooding Professor Brody.

Daniel Deep hadn't joined them for the meal, which

wasn't particularly surprising given the circumstances. His PA Emily had said it was because of another business meeting, which might have been true, but Cullen doubted it.

In fact, he wondered if they would see Deep again on the trip.

After all, he'd said his piece yesterday evening during dinner.

'Are you going on the bus tour?' Hillary asked the guests next to and across from her. As well as passing on the message about Deep's absence, Emily had also announced an afternoon mini-bus trip up across the top of the peaks that encircled the Loch.

There were a few nods, but a notable shake of the head from Professor Brody and from Joseph, who had been subdued since joining them at the table.

'You feeling okay?' Cullen asked Joseph, who hadn't yet touched his food.

Joseph shook his head, before pushing himself away from the table. 'I need to get some more fresh air.'

'Too much to drink last night?' Hilary asked, as the group watched Joseph leave the room.

'Something like that,' Cullen confirmed, remembering back to the conversation he had interrupted outside the washroom.

'Some lungfuls of that Highland air will do him the world of good,' Hilary noted. 'I can see why he doesn't want to do the mini-bus thing - probably for the best.'

They returned to eating. Once or twice, Cullen spotted Professor Brody looking at him, as if he was about to say something, but deciding against it. Once the table was cleared, the group parted company, with Cullen heading back towards his room.

He was intercepted at the top of the stairs by the Professor.

'Detective Cullen,' Brody said, jogging up the last few steps to catch up with him. 'Can I have a word?'

Cullen noticed he was holding a piece of paper down by his side. 'Sure. What's up?'

'Do you know where Daniel Deep is?' he asked unexpectedly.

'Deep?' Cullen replied, wondering why the professor would think that he'd have any special intelligence about Deep's movements. 'No idea, I'm afraid.'

Brody paused, disappointment evident. 'It's just that, I have this.' He waved the paper. 'And I have a narrowing window of opportunity. I don't want to leave it until we board the train - it will be too late.'

Cullen eyed the paper.

'It's an agreement,' Brody explained. 'For Deep to sign. It commits him to taking genuine action to clean up his mess in the town of Hope, both in terms of the environmental impact and also the potential health effects of the train derailment. I've run this past lawyers, and although it's a brief document, it's water-tight. I just need his signature.'

'Don't you mean his agreement?' Cullen replied.

'Yes, yes, of course. His agreement, with his signature as evidence and as legal proof.'

'Do you think he'll agree to it?'

'I really don't know. But after what he said yesterday, about making things right, there's a chance. I don't know if I believe him, to be honest, but I reckon that this is the best shot to get something for the people of Hope, right here, right now.'

'You're a good man,' Cullen commented.

'It won't mean anything if I don't get that signature.'

Cullen nodded. 'His private study is downstairs, towards the back of the castle. I met him there this morning - it looked like a likely place to do a business meeting. There was a computer in there and working desk. He might not be there, but there's a chance.'

Brody broke out into a broad grin and patted Cullen on the arm. 'You're a good man, too, Inspector.'

'I try and sometimes don't fail,' Cullen noted.

'Don't we all, Inspector, don't we all.'

'Well good luck with it,' Cullen said. 'I genuinely hope you get what you came here for. Look forward to catching up later about it.'

Cullen made to turn, but Brody called out. 'There's one more thing.'

'Sure.'

Brody held up the paper again. 'I need a witness for the signature. An independent witness. And I thought an officer of the law would be a perfect candidate.'

~

CULLEN ACCOMPANIED Brody back down the stairs and towards Daniel Deep's study. Cullen sensed Brody's nervousness as they approached the door.

'I think you're right,' Cullen reassured the professor, 'this is your best chance.'

Brody nodded. 'I just know how unpredictable he is. I know too much about him to be that confident, when I really think about it.'

Cullen nodded his understanding.

Brody continued, in hushed tones. 'I mean, the things he's

done in the past, the way he's behaved, can he have changed that much?'

'I really don't know,' Cullen admitted, thinking back to Deep's revelation about his prognosis. If the professor knew the full story, then maybe he would be more confident about Deep's apparent transformation. 'But I guess there's only one way to find out.'

'Indeed,' Brody said, straightening up his frame as they reached the door, mentally preparing himself for the imminent challenge.

'Ready?' Cullen said, about to knock.

'As I'll ever be.'

Cullen went to knock, but paused as a raised voice came from behind the door.

It was Daniel Deep. The door was thick, so it was hard to make out what he was saying.

You said you would support me!

Cullen assumed he was on a call, but without warning, the door was yanked open and Emily fled past them, hurrying along the corridor. Such was her desire for flight, that she didn't seem to have even noticed the two men standing right outside.

'Maybe now's not a good time after all,' Brody noted, as they watched Emily disappear around the corner.

'Maybe you're right,' Cullen replied, wondering.

But they'd already been spotted.

'Gentlemen,' Deep said, standing at the door and looking completely unflustered by the apparent altercation with his personal assistant. 'How can I help you?'

Brody looked at Cullen, then back at Deep. 'I was hoping you might sign this,' he said, holding up the piece of paper.

Deep's eyes narrowed as he took hold of the agreement and began to read.

'You expect me to sign this without consulting my legal team first?' Deep said, after looking at both sides of the document.

'I guess so,' Brody replied.

Deep looked at the agreement again, turning it over a couple of times, thinking.

'I'd be happy to talk through any of it,' Brody tried. 'Hopefully it's pretty self-explanatory.'

'Fine,' Deep said. 'It's fine. Let me grab a pen. Come in and we'll get this done.'

Brody looked at Cullen again with surprised joy behind his eyes as they followed Deep into the room and up to the desk. Deep already had a pen in hand, and was signing and dating the document. He slid the paper across to the two men and placed the pen next to them.

'I assume you sign that, Inspector,' he said.

Cullen added his signature and dated.

'And there you go,' Deep said, passing the agreement back to Brody. 'Signed, sealed and delivered.'

Brody held the paper, scarcely able to believe that it had been so easy. 'Thank you.'

'My pleasure,' Deep replied. 'Now gentlemen, if you would excuse me, I've got something urgent to attend to.'

'I can't believe that just happened,' Brody admitted, as he and Cullen walked back towards the main entrance. 'I must admit, I'm a little stunned. I mean, I thought there was a chance, but...'

'Certainly a great result,' Cullen replied absentmindedly. He was thinking about the heated discussion they had interrupted between Deep and Emily. Maybe it was nothing, but she had certainly looked shaken, and he wondered what it had been about and how she was.

There was something about it that really bothered him. Maybe the way that Deep had seemed totally unaffected while she had been in pieces.

He would endeavour to find her.

37

Previously

Daniel Deep sat in his opulent study, surrounded by his vast collection of model trains. He watched as they zoomed on autopilot around the tracks, criss-crossing in between one another. One train passed closely across another, but there was no danger of any accidents here; everything was timed to absolute precision and that particular manoeuvre happened several hundred times a day as the trains operated from morning until night.

The specially designed room was vast and full of the miniature electric trains and the detailed landscape that they travelled over. There were half a dozen model stations, each complete with the usual station facilities and the passengers ever-waiting for the next arrival. Close to him was a beach zone, with actual water lapping across towards the sunbathers, and a train line running behind. Across on the other side of the room a man-made, fake-snow topped mountain range towered halfway towards the high ceiling, with a track snaking its way around and inside it.

He sat forward and watched the mountain locomotive climb towards the peak.

This room was his sanctuary.

It was a place he could go to get away from everything. He had always been fascinated by the intricate details of these tiny locomotives, ever since his father had bought him that first oval track which they would play with in the loft for what seemed like hours on end.

As a child he'd loved the way the engines zipped along the tracks with such precision and grace.

They had so many happy times in that attic space, his father and him, lost among the sights, sounds and smells of their expanding model railway. He remembered much laughter between them. Such good times.

Before the floods of tears.

After his father had died, he would spend many hours up there alone in the darkness of the attic, lights off as the trains ran, listening to the sound of them as they made their way along the tracks. He cried and cried, ignoring the calls of his mother from down below, refusing to open the hatch.

He knew what they'd said about him then. And he knew what they'd said about him now. They'd ridiculed him for his love of model railways, as if he was just a big kid. And yes, there was something childlike and innocent about his obsession, he recognised that.

But today, as he sat hunched, surveying his creation, Deep's thoughts were far from innocent. His mind was consumed by negativity; frustration and anger at what was happening to him.

How could he take back control?

Power and control was what he thrived on for all these years, manipulating those around him to do his bidding - by persuasion, coercion or force, it really didn't matter.

The seeds had been formed in that attic, and he'd exited it with a new determination to not only be the best person he could be, but to be better than the rest, to succeed where others would fail.

To never lose anything again, to anyone or anything.

But suddenly, inexplicably, things had changed.

As he tinkered with the tiny tracks and switches via the control panel in front of him, his mind began to race with possibilities. He had always been a man who loved to plan, to strategise, to find new ways to exert his influence to ever further reaches.

He powered up the train that had been waiting along the bottom edge of the room. The powerful maroon and gold engine, pulling ten plush carriages, edged forwards.

Deep Sleeper One.

In just a few weeks' time, the train would make its maiden voyage from the heart of London to the wondrous Scottish Highlands, heralding the dawn of a new age of luxury train travel that would spread across Continental Europe and then the world.

At least that had been the plan.

Anger flared again at the realisation of how this dream was now shattered.

With a flick of his wrist, Deep sent the train whizzing along the tracks, twisting and turning as it wound its way through the miniature landscape. He watched it go, a sinister smile playing at the corners of his mouth. Rising victorious from his childhood trauma, Deep had sought to shape the world in his image, to bend it to his will, and he had done just that.

He could do it again.

As he continued to play with his trains, he began to mentally rehearse the plan that would change everything.

He would go down in history.

He knew that there would be obstacles along the way, that there would be those who would try to stop him. But Deep was a man who never backed down from a challenge. He was determined to see his vision through to the end, no matter what the cost.

Deep disengaged the automatic safety function on the train set and pressed down harder on the controls to send the model of Deep Sleeper hurtling forwards, faster and faster, twisting one way then another, until it left the tracks through sheer velocity, just as it was approaching a viaduct. The engine corkscrewed across the bridge, and it and the carriages it was pulling plunged into the water below, with a satisfying splash and sparks fizzing in the water.

'That was perfect,' he smiled, as the engine, submerged, flashed once more before dying.

And as he sat there, his mind buzzing with ideas and possibilities, he knew that the world would never be the same again. He would leave a shocking legacy that would far outlast his own life.

He was back in control, and ready to make his move.

PART IV

38

Present Day

Despite Cullen's best efforts, he had no luck in tracking down Emily Parker. Even when the group arrived back at Tulloch station, at eight thirty, and boarded Deep Sleeper, there was no sign of her or Daniel Deep.

Cullen settled back into his cabin - the same one he had been allocated on the journey up - and kept one eye out on the platform to see if he could spot the personal assistant.

Then he heard the helicopter, and stepping back outside saw it touch down to the west of the train station, probably in one of the open fields. Cullen ignored the efforts of the station staff to usher him back onto the train, keen to be there when she arrived. But after a few minutes, one of Deep's bodyguards wouldn't take no for an answer, and Cullen retreated back onboard, a little frustrated but determined to get to Emily sooner rather than later.

Just half an hour after they had boarded, they moved off,

the powerful locomotive hauling the carriages and its passengers away from their temporary Highland home and back down South.

Fifteen minutes into the journey, Cullen decided to take his chance, and headed along the train's length, his eyes out for Emily. Cursing himself that he didn't know which cabin she was staying in, he followed logic by focussing on the rear of the train; Daniel Deep's quarters were at the front, and maybe they'd arranged it so that both ends were occupied by key members of Deep's entourage.

Cullen passed through the observation car, occupied by several guests but none that he had got to know well, before reaching the final carriage. The approach to it did resemble the look of Deep's private suite at the train's front; including the presence of a bodyguard.

'Can I help you, Detective?' the guard said. Cullen recognised him as one of the men who had saved his life earlier that morning.

'I was hoping to speak with Emily,' Cullen said breezily. 'If she has a few minutes spare.'

The guard considered the request.

'Thank you again for this morning,' Cullen said, cutting into the guard's thoughts. 'You guys literally saved my life. I wouldn't be here if it wasn't for your actions.'

The guard grinned. 'Don't mention it. More than happy to be of assistance. After all, you were trying to save the Boss.'

'Yes, I was.'

Cullen let the comment hang, waiting to see if his tactic would work.

'I'll ask her,' the guard said at last. 'But she did say she wanted some time alone. Just a second.'

'Much appreciated.'

The guard ducked in through the door and emerged just a few moments later. 'You can go in,' he said.

Cullen nodded his thanks, and before the guard could change his mind, squeezed past him into the room. The suite was very much like Daniel Deep's at the front of the train, although it had been kitted out in a more homely way.

Emily was standing by the panoramic window, gazing out, and only turned around ever so slightly to say hello, before returning to her thoughts.

'I came to see how you were,' Cullen said, deciding that he couldn't afford to dance around the issue for fear that their conversation might get cut short. 'You were upset earlier, back at the castle. I wondered if you needed someone to talk to, about what happened.'

'You don't know what happened,' she stated, not turning around. 'Or what's happening.'

'No, I don't,' Cullen said, his interest certainly piqued by that last comment. 'What *is* happening, Emily?'

Emily turned around, her face drained of its colour. She looked full of the world's problems. It set Cullen on edge.

Could whatever this was have implications for all of them?

He watched Emily pace around the carriage, arms crossed in front of her. There was no attempt to put on a brave face.

She looked tortured.

'Emily? What's going on?'

She stopped her pacing, her mouth opening as if to say something. But no words came out, and instead she gazed up at the ceiling, hugging herself tightly.

'Daniel told me about his illness,' Cullen said, in an attempt to kickstart the conversation.

This got her interest. 'Did he?' she asked, surprised, looking across to him.

'This morning, after what happened on the Loch, he told me about the tumour; and about the prognosis.'

Emily looked confused. 'What happened on the Loch?'

This time it was Cullen who was taken by surprise. He'd assumed that as his PA, Emily would know everything that was going on, particularly something that had been so serious.

'He got into trouble while swimming,' Cullen revealed.

'Trouble?'

Cullen decided to pull no punches. 'He nearly drowned. They think he had a seizure, in the middle of the Loch, during his early morning swim. He had to be rescued by his guards.'

Emily blinked in disbelief, as if she was still processing the information, but her expression quickly turned darker. 'He didn't mention a thing,' she said to herself. 'Nothing.' She looked at Cullen. 'He really nearly died?'

'Yes.' He didn't add that he himself had also very nearly joined the casualty list in his fruitless attempt to save Deep.

She shook her head again. 'He doesn't care about me,' she said, speaking her thoughts out loud. 'If he really loved me...'

Cullen's ears pricked up at that.

They were in a relationship?

It was hard to know where to tread with this, with the conversation taking an unexpected turn. Cullen had wanted to check on Emily's well-being, but now he was here, it felt like there was something more, something waiting to be uncovered.

You don't know what happened...or what's happening.

Or what's happening.

'Are you and Daniel together?'

She laughed bitterly. 'I thought so,' she said. She shook her head. 'But I think he's just using me.'

'Using you for what?'

'For his own gain,' she spat, 'like he does with everyone else; like he's always done.'

'Why do you think he's using you?' Cullen probed. He still didn't really know where he was going with this particular line of enquiry, but experience had taught him that often just setting off with some questions could lead to the most surprising, and insightful of destinations.

That was the skill and magic of investigative questioning.

Words could unlock the strongest of doors.

'If he genuinely cared about me, he would tell me the truth,' she replied. 'And he would listen to me.'

'Is that why you were upset this morning; because he wasn't listening to you?'

She put a hand to her forehead, gripping her temple hard. 'What have I done?'

Cullen resisted the temptation to step closer. He still had no clue as to what she was talking about; whether this was just a domestic incident between her and Deep, or if it was something more worrying.

But the truth was nearly within reach; he sensed it.

Grab for it too quickly though, and it could slip through your fingers.

'What's going on, Emily?' he asked, with a little more authority but still treading lightly. 'Is it something to do with this weekend? This trip?'

Her reaction told Cullen he was on the right lines, although she said nothing.

Thoughts were flashing through Cullen's head - none of them good.

What was all this about?

'Please, Emily,' he tried again. This time he ventured a couple of steps forward. 'Whatever is happening here, just tell me. I can help.'

'I should have done something sooner,' she said. 'I tried, this morning, I tried.'

'Daniel invited all these people who he had crossed paths with, who he had wronged. Joseph, Professor Brody, Hillary, Stephen Dormer. Why? Was it really to make amends?'

She shook her head.

'Then why?'

'They should have let him drown,' she said finally.

'What?'

This time the words came more cautiously, as if she appreciated the gravity of what she was saying. But there was total certainty in what she said. 'They should have let him drown. Maybe that's what was meant to happen - fate was trying to intervene.'

'I really don't understand.'

Emily looked straight at Cullen, her eyes wet with tears. 'He's going to kill us all.'

39

Cullen stood there in shock, adrenaline coursing through his body. 'He's trying to kill us?'

Emily put a hand to her head again. 'He's been planning it for a few weeks,' she said, as if the horror of the situation was only just dawning on her. He's got it all worked out.'

'What's he planning to do, Emily?'

She looked like she was going to be physically sick.

'Emily, you've got to tell me. I can help.'

'It's too late!' she shouted, panic evident in her voice. 'There's nothing we can do to stop it now. Nothing!'

There was a knock on the door. 'Is everything okay, Ms Parker?' the bodyguard asked through the door. He would have heard her shouting.

'Yes, fine,' she shouted back. 'I'm fine.'

Cullen was relieved when the guard seemed to take her word for it. It would complicate things if they'd been interrupted. He needed to calm Emily down, and extract the truth from her, quickly.

He moved across to her. 'I can help,' he said kindly, maintaining eye contact.

She shook her head, her eyes closing and a hand across her mouth.

'It's never too late,' Cullen said, 'to try and make things right.'

Sometimes it was just about finding the right words, and putting them in the right order, at the right time.

Emily opened her eyes and nodded, already seeming calmer and more focussed.

'He's planning to crash the train,' she said, breathing slowly to calm herself some more. 'Derail it.'

'*Derail* the train? How?'

'The viaduct. The train will come off the tracks if the approach is too fast. He's worked it out, planned it down to the finest detail. The train will hit the bend just before the bridge at eighty eight miles an hour, veer off the tracks, and plunge into the valley.'

'My God.'

The pieces fell into place like a macabre jigsaw puzzle, and Cullen's mind raced with the gravity of the situation. Deep Sleeper was not just a luxurious train; it was a death trap hurtling towards disaster. Daniel Deep's invitation to his enemies, his attempts at redemption, it was all a carefully crafted ruse to bring them together for their final act.

Cullen looked out of the window at the countryside whizzing by. The train must have been doing at least eighty already. He did some calculations. They'd been travelling for around twenty five minutes, and the viaduct wasn't that far away; when they'd crossed it on the outward journey, during breakfast with Zack, it wasn't that long before they'd started slowing for their approach to Tulloch.

'How long?' Cullen said, desperately thinking through his options, 'until the bridge? Thirty minutes?'

Emily looked at her watch. 'Twenty five.'

'Okay,' Cullen said, thinking as fast as he could about the options. But before he did anything else, he pulled out his mobile.

Thank goodness there was a signal.

He speed-dialled the British Transport Police's emergency control centre, a staff-only number that could be used to request emergency assistance across the BTP network.

'British Transport Police,' came the speedy answer. 'How can I help?'

Cullen gave his name and number, then hastily explained the situation, answering the operator's calm questions as fully as he could.

He'd have been foolish not to have called them, but he couldn't see how they would be able to do anything, given the deadline they would be working to and the complexity of the scenario.

Then something came to him.

'I've just had a thought,' Cullen said. 'Whether there's a way to divert the train away from the viaduct; if there are any points up ahead that could take the train onto another line?'

If that was a possibility, then it would surely be the number one option. They would still need to deal with the train, and Daniel Deep, because even on a new line an out of control train would eventually spell disaster, but it would remove the urgent threat from the bridge and buy them a little time.

'I'm sure that possibility will be explored urgently,' the operator said.

The more minds that were on this, the better. Even as the

call was continuing, the national alert would have gone out, and people nationwide - some of the most talented and dedicated men and women Cullen had ever had the good fortune to work alongside - would be mobilising.

'We'll do all we can,' the operator continued. 'We'll throw everything at it.'

'I know you will,' Cullen said, already thinking beyond the call now that he had informed the authorities.

The clock was ticking.

'Good luck,' the operator said. 'We're here on standby whenever you need it. And we'll be back in touch within the next ten minutes.'

Ten minutes closer to the bridge...

Twenty short minutes from the abyss.

'Can they help?' Emily asked anxiously as Cullen ended the call. 'What are they going to do?'

'I'm not sure,' Cullen replied. 'But they'll try their best.'

Cullen thought through the best options for stopping the train.

There was one obvious action. 'The driver,' Cullen said. 'Is there a way we can communicate with the driver? An intercom? He must know what is happening? Surely he doesn't want to die?'

Emily looked sick at his suggestion.

'What? What is it?' Cullen asked.

'There is no driver,' Emily stated.

40

Cullen was left blindsided by Emily's revelation. 'There isn't a driver?'

'Deep Sleeper One is a driverless train,' she said.

'What? But the authorities, they would need to agree to it running, and it's not been done before, there's no national agreement.'

'The authorities don't know,' Emily replied.

'But they didn't spot this before the journey? Surely in the pre-checks, the engineers would have flagged it.' It didn't make any sense - there would have been a thorough examination of the train before it was given permission to run on the UK rail network.

'It's a hybrid vehicle,' she replied. 'It can run traditionally, with driver operation, or it can switch to autopilot, and run according to a pre-programmed route.'

'And the UK authorities were told that it would run traditionally?'

'Yes,' she confirmed. 'And it did run with a driver, on the outward leg.'

It all made sense.

'Where's the driver now?'

'I don't know,' she said. 'He left on Saturday morning. He was told that another driver was taking the train back down.'

'Damn it.' He'd briefly thought that if the driver had been on board, they could have been enlisted to take control of the vehicle.

Cullen looked at his watch.

'We need to sound the emergency alarm,' he said, kicking himself for not thinking of that sooner. The shock of the situation had momentarily stifled his thinking, but he was already scanning the carriage for a button or lever. 'That usually initiates the emergency brake.'

'It's right outside,' Emily said, brightening. They headed for the door, but just as Cullen emerged from the carriage, the red alarm light began flashing on the wall in the corridor.

Someone else must have got there before them...

Worryingly, the train didn't appear to be slowing.

Before Cullen had time to think what this meant, Karl came running through into the compartment.

'We know what's happening,' he said, breathlessly. It was disconcerting to see the usually unflappable Karl struggling for words. 'I've just tried to stop the train with the emergency button, but it hasn't worked.'

'How did you find out?' Cullen asked, 'did Deep tell you?'

Karl shook his head. 'Vincent heard you guys talking a few minutes ago,' he panted. 'Came to let me know. I've just ran the length of the train.'

'Can you think of anything else we can do?' Cullen said.

'I was planning to ask you the same,' Karl replied.

Cullen looked at Emily, who shook her head despondently.

'Well we need to do something,' Cullen said. Looking out of the window, it was clear that the train was not slowing. 'We need to speak to Deep, try and convince him to call this all off.'

'He won't change his mind,' Emily stated. 'In the past few weeks - I don't know if it's the effect of the brain tumour - I've noticed he's become even more self-obsessed, more driven; his mind won't be turned, he won't be persuaded to do something that he doesn't want to do.'

'We *have* to try,' Cullen shot back. 'There are thirty or so people on this train who have,' he looked at his watch again, 'about twenty minutes to live unless we can talk Deep around.'

Emily nodded her understanding.

'I tried to speak to him just a few minutes ago,' Karl revealed. 'He's locked the door and isn't answering his phone or the intercom.'

'We *need* to get him to listen,' Cullen said, with little choice but to reject the idea that this was an impossible task.

'Agreed,' Karl said.

'What about the other passengers?' Cullen suddenly thought. 'Do any of them know?'

'No,' Karl confirmed. Just Vincent and me - not even the rest of the security team. I've put out the word that the emergency alarm is a test.'

'That's good. We will need to tell them, at some point soon, but for now, I don't want twenty panicking passengers adding to the situation. And let's turn the alarm off. We know it's not working.'

'Understood,' Karl said, evidently comfortable with following Cullen's orders in this unfolding scenario.

Cullen thought of Zack, deciding he wouldn't tell him

either yet. They needed to focus, and the more people who they introduced into this, the more chance their attention could be taken away from the task at hand.

Act now, explain later.

'Let's go and speak to Daniel Deep,' Cullen said, already setting off down the carriage.

The other two followed without question.

41

Cullen made his way along the train, trying his very best to keep a poker face as he passed guests. The alarm had been turned off, but it was likely that the recently-flashing lights had unnerved some of the passengers and they would be on high alert for anything usual occurring.

'Everything okay, Detective?' Professor Brody asked as the three of them moved through the observation carriage.

'All fine,' Cullen said, feeling a little guilty at the deception. The Professor might have been a help - he certainly had a sharp brain - but it was just too risky to tell people about what was happening on a pick-and-choose basis.

'Good, good,' the Professor answered, watching with interest as Karl and Emily followed.

Cullen passed through the main passenger carriages, and fortunately didn't encounter anyone. So he picked up the pace, half-jogging past the cabins. Emily and Karl kept up with him, sharing his sense of urgency.

He slowed down again upon reaching the restaurant

carriage. It was full of diners, some with glasses of champagne in hand, others enjoying the high quality cuisine.

Their pleasant evening was in all likelihood about to be rudely interrupted.

He exchanged smiles with the guests, including Hilary and Deep's cousin, Stephen Dormer, as they passed through.

'Evening,' came the refrain from several of the diners.

There didn't seem to be any sense of concern here regarding the activation of the alarm. It appeared the explanation of a test had been swallowed whole.

'Detective Cullen!' Joseph said, standing at the bar with a deep blue cocktail in hand. He held the drink up. 'Cheers for a bright new future!' he said, taking a sip and letting out a satisfied sigh.

Cullen mustered a tight smile back, but didn't stop, instead moving out of the carriage and past the kitchen zone towards Deep's quarters.

'Daniel,' Cullen said, knocking on the door. 'It's Paul Cullen. I need to speak with you, urgently.'

There was no answer as Emily and Karl joined him at his shoulder, their faces full of anxiety.

'That's what he's been like - refusing to talk,' Karl said.

Cullen tried again. 'Daniel,' he said, louder and more insistent this time. 'You need to let me in.'

Surprisingly the door clicked open, and Deep was standing there, one hand against the frame.

'Just you,' he said, addressing Cullen. 'The others wait outside.'

Cullen turned to Emily and Karl and they nodded.

At that, Deep opened the door a little more and Cullen stepped through.

Deep was quick to lock the door behind him.

Suppressing a surge of adrenaline, Cullen stepped forward, his voice steady yet laced with urgency. 'Daniel, what are you doing? We need to stop this madness!'

Deep stood in the room's centre, hands on hips, his eyes burning with determination and challenge.

'In under twenty minutes, this train and everyone on board will go down in history,' he stated. 'It will be remembered for ever.'

'Tell me what this is all about,' Cullen said, trying with some difficulty to take a diplomatic tone. The only possible chance of success here was to try and reason with Deep; he wouldn't be able to fight his way out of this.

Deep smiled. 'I expected this,' he said. 'And you really haven't disappointed, Detective Chief Inspector Cullen.'

'I don't understand.'

'Well, here you are,' he smiled, 'trying to save the day - playing your part perfectly.'

'This isn't a game,' Cullen shot back. 'People's lives are at risk. In twenty minutes, everyone on board here will be dead. Do you want that?'

'I want to be remembered!' Deep spat. 'I will *not* be forgotten, and consigned to history!' He checked himself, as if shocked by the intensity of his own emotions. He turned on the spot, battling with himself, anger boiling.

Cullen sensed an opportunity. 'You really want to be remembered for mass murder? For killing innocent people?'

'If that's what it takes to live forever!' he shouted. He pointed towards Cullen, his face full of anguish. 'All my life, I have been so focussed, so dedicated, to be the best I can be, to be *the* best. To succeed where others have failed. To rise above the ordinary. This thing,' he spat, jabbing at his temple, 'this invader inside my head. It thought it could beat me, bring me down, destroy me and wipe me off the face of the earth. But it can't! I took back control, and I will win! Do you understand?'

'There is another way,' Cullen said. 'You have a legacy. People will remember you. Do what you said yesterday - spend the rest of your time doing good things, making amends.'

'I don't need to make amends for anything,' he replied. 'You know who needed to make amends? My father for dying and leaving me alone in that attic. I was so desperately unhappy and scared after he abandoned me. I only had my trains...'

'I'm sorry for what happened to you,' was Cullen's genuine reply. 'I can't imagine how that must have...'

'Don't,' Deep cut across him, wagging a finger. 'Don't you dare try and empathise with my situation and paint me as a victim. I am *not* a victim!'

'But the guests aboard Deep Sleeper will be,' Cullen said. 'So will their families, their friends, when they find out their loves ones are gone.'

'I hand-chose each and every one of them,' Deep dismissed. 'Their fate was sealed from the moment they accepted my invitation. A few lucky ones refused, and they've been rewarded with their lives. But this lot, they had a choice and they have lost.'

'What about Emily?' Cullen asked. 'You're happy for her to die too, are you? She really cares about you.'

Deep was impassive, but Cullen wasn't about to stop there.

'What has Emily done wrong?'

'She opened herself up to trusting another human being,'

Deep replied. 'And in a way I trusted her too; until this morning.'

'The argument? In your office?'

'She thought she could change my mind,' he shrugged. 'I've heard that women believe they have particular abilities when it comes to influencing the actions of the men they love. Still, she tried to convince me to abort my plans, but didn't warn you or the others until it was too late.'

'You believe she loves you, but you're still prepared to do this?'

'She *thinks* she loves me.'

Cullen paused for thought. This conversation wasn't really going anywhere, and the minutes were passing by.

'What makes you think that by crashing this train you'll be remembered forever?' Cullen said, trying to take a different tack, given the increasing urgency of the situation. 'It will be a big news story, yes, for a few days, maybe a couple of weeks. But no-one will know the truth behind what happened; that it was all part of your plan. They will assume that there was some kind of malfunction, and it was an accident.'

Deep smiled. 'I'm sure you've already alerted the authorities and told them all about my plans.'

Cullen was about to consider a lie when out of the window a police helicopter appeared, flying alongside the train at a safe distance.

'Aha!' Deep shouted with glee, clasping his hands together whilst moving over to the window. 'I see your friends have arrived.' He turned to Cullen. 'I wonder how they are planning to stop the train? Maybe fly their flimsy helicopter in front of my powerful train and try to derail it?' he mocked. 'That would cause a lot of mess.'

Cullen eyed the helicopter. They would be assessing the situation visually. And probably despairing at their lack of options.

'They won't report the full story,' Cullen said in desperation. 'No-one will know you were behind all this.'

Deep wasn't having any of it. 'You need to try harder than that, Detective. And anyway, the news is already out there. Most people on this train might be gloriously oblivious to their impending doom, but the world does know.'

'How?'

Deep pulled out his phone. 'Live stream,' he revealed. 'Just before you came knocking.' His pressed at the device. 'Wow,' he said, grinning, 'my notifications are off the scale!'

'I'm not sure you want this to happen,' Cullen said, ignoring Deep's social media boasts. 'Otherwise, why invite me along? Why choose to have a police officer on board?'

Deep slipped his phone back into his pocket. 'I like to win, and I *always* do win; but winning without competition is just so unsatisfying,' he explained.

'So that's why you wanted me here, to try and stop you?'

'Try, yes.'

'Why me?'

'I already told you,' Deep said. 'I admire you, Detective. The investigations you've led, on the UK's railways, I've read all about them. After that first story I saw in the newspaper, I kind of got a little obsessed with you and your team.'

Cullen suddenly thought of his young friend, who was still completely unaware of what was happening. 'And Zack. Why invite Zack along? He's just a young kid.'

Deep shrugged. 'I like Zack.'

'Then why?'

'His connection to you,' Deep said. 'I knew you had

worked together from my reading of your cases. Indeed there is a friendship there, isn't there? Having Zack on board just helped to ensure that you would join me.'

Cullen looked at his watch again. There was less than twenty minutes until they reached the bridge. He couldn't even think about what to say, he was running out of track both figuratively and literally. 'Please, Daniel, just put a stop to this.'

'That's your job not mine,' Deep challenged back. 'There's still time, Detective Cullen, but not much of it.'

42

Cullen left Deep and headed back outside, where he found Emily and Karl waiting.

'There's no convincing him,' Cullen reported back. 'But we need to do something.'

'What?' Emily said, panic in her voice as Karl looked on solemnly. 'What can we do?'

'We need to tell everyone,' Cullen said. 'All the guests and staff. Move everyone to the very back of the train - to your carriage - and stay there with them.'

'We tell them they're about to die?' Emily replied disbelievingly. 'But they'll panic, won't they? How do we deal with that?'

'We'll deal with it,' Karl said calmly.

'Good man,' Cullen said. He turned to Emily. 'You've got an important role to play, Emily. The passengers trust you; you can help to keep them as calm as possible.'

Emily nodded uncertainly.

'You can do it,' Karl assured her. 'Let's go and get this done.'

'One thing,' Cullen said. Then he paused. He was going to request that Zack came forward to join him. But although he would value his input, it would place him at greater risk, should he fail to avert the impending disaster. 'Tell Zack from me, I'm going to do whatever it takes.'

'What are you going to do?' Emily replied. 'What *can* you do?'

'I don't know,' Cullen admitted. He thought again. 'Is there a way of overriding the train? Of taking back control?'

'There will be,' she confirmed. 'But without Daniel's help, I don't know how to override the system.'

Again, their fate fell to the belligerent billionaire.

'Is there anyone else who would know how to override the system?' Cullen asked, desperately searching for options. 'Anyone? Surely the people that designed and built it. Can we get in touch with them?'

'I wouldn't know where to start,' Emily admitted.

'The driver!' Cullen said, snapping his fingers at the belated brainwave. 'The driver who operated the train on the way here. He would know, wouldn't he?'

Emily brightened. 'Yes, yes he would!'

'Please tell me you have his contact details,' Cullen said, not quite daring to believe that he had found a way through this.

'I have,' Emily said. 'I have!'

She scrambled for her phone, scrolling rapidly through her contacts until she reached the name she was looking for.

'Thomas Wellens,' she announced, passing the phone to Cullen. 'Thomas Wellens, the driver on the way here.'

'Fantastic,' Cullen said, copying the number across to his phone. He handed Emily back her device.

Suddenly Emily's face fell. 'The driver's cab, it will be locked.'

Cullen hadn't even thought of that possibility, but it was pretty obvious. 'You've not got keys?'

'Only Daniel.'

'Okay,' Cullen said. 'Let me deal with it. Now you two, get those passengers to the back of the train.'

'Can I ask why?' Karl said. 'Why the back?'

'I have a plan,' Cullen replied. 'You're just going to have to trust me. And cross your fingers.'

43

'You're back,' Deep said, as Cullen re-entered his carriage. 'Any bright ideas about what to do? I see your friends in the helicopter are still keeping us company. Hope they've got their video running - should be quite a sight. Fifteen minutes to go.'

Cullen ignored the jibes. 'The cab,' he said. 'I need the keys.'

'It's pointless,' Deep replied. 'The train is on autopilot, as I'm sure Emily has explained to you. There's no way for you to stop it.'

'Just give me the keys.'

Deep smiled. 'You're wasting your time,' he said, moving across to the corner of the room and grabbing something small from a side table, which he threw in Cullen's direction. 'But I want to give you every chance, just for the fun of it.'

Cullen's reactions were good, and he plucked the fob from the air. 'Thank you,' he said, the security device safely in his hand. 'Look,' he tried one last time, 'I can do this with you, or

I can do this without you. Choose to end this now and you'll still have your legacy.'

'Good luck, Detective,' Deep said. 'You'll need it.'

'As you wish.'

Cullen turned and headed out, towards the very front of Deep Sleeper, his determination to succeed against all odds never stronger.

44

Cullen hurried along the corridor, which narrowed past Deep's quarters, and approached the door to Deep Sleeper's cab. Using the newly acquired security fob, he swiped through and entered.

He took in the scene. The train's control room was more like an aircraft cockpit. A large, sweeping console of buttons and screens spread out before him and it was clear just how much the one-time freight vehicle had been modified by Deep.

Dead ahead of him, through the front windows, Cullen saw the track rushing ominously towards them.

They were speeding to oblivion.

He brought his phone up towards him and was about to call the driver, when another call came through.

'Cullen speaking.'

The emergency response operator gave a quick update, promising that they were running through all possible options, but that unfortunately there was no opportunity to divert the train. Such was Cullen's desire for urgency, he didn't waste any time by telling them their idea of contacting the driver, and instead ended the call with the promise of another update should the situation change.

With one more look out of the front window, he hit dial on the driver's number.

It was ringing.

'Come on, come on, pick up...pick up...'

There was no answer.

'Damn it!' The call had gone through to answerphone. 'Thomas, if you get this, please call back now. There's an emergency on Deep Sleeper. Please call back urgently.'

Cullen cut the call and immediately redialled.

Still just ringing.

'Pick up the phone! Pick up the phone!'

Again it went through to the phone's messaging service.

Cullen gazed in horror at the track ahead. It might have just been his imagination, but it seemed the train was increasing its speed.

He dialled again.

And again.

There was only around ten minutes...

And then...

'Hello?'

'Thomas? Thomas Wellens?'

'Speaking...'

Cullen actually laughed in relief. 'Thank God. Look, I really need your help. I'm on board Deep Sleeper, and I'm hoping you can save some lives here, including mine.'

45

Cullen explained the situation to the horrified driver, who confirmed Emily's story that he had been told his one-way assignment up to Scotland was because there was another driver booked for the return leg. Recognising the dire straits they were in, the driver then quickly but carefully talked through the instructions while Cullen listened intently.

'And once you disengage the autopilot, the locomotive will revert to manual control,' the driver explained. 'I could talk you through how to slow the train, but the easiest and quickest thing to do would be to engage the train's emergency brakes. That's a straight forward operation, a double-press of the red emergency stop button, and it will bring the train to a controlled stop.'

'And if it doesn't stop in time? I was thinking, if there might be a way to disconnect the rear carriages - the rest of the passengers are back there.'

'That would be possible, but shouldn't be necessary,' the driver replied, 'given what you've told me about how far you are from the bridge, the train will stop in time. But if it doesn't stop completely, it should slow it enough for a safe crossing. Are you ready?'

'Let's do it,' Cullen said, feeling confident at last that everything was going to be alright.

Even though it still felt much too close for comfort.

'I underestimated you,' a voice said from behind him.

Cullen turned, phone still to his ear, as he watched Daniel Deep enter the cab.

'You're talking to the driver,' Deep stated. 'I guess it was an obvious option. Please put the phone down.'

'I can't do that,' Cullen replied.

Deep flew at him, knocking the phone from his hand as Cullen sought to dodge the assault. Deep went for the device, where it lay wedged under the driver's seat, but Cullen rugby tackled him, driving him into the side of the cab with a heavy thud.

Cullen held him against the side. 'Stop this now,' Cullen demanded, as Deep struggled to break free. 'It's over.'

'Never!'

In a swift motion, Deep sidestepped Cullen's hold, delivering a powerful blow that sent the detective crashing to the ground, winded. Pain surged through Cullen's body, though his determination remained. But as he tried to scramble to his feet, Deep kicked up into his chest, before planting a hard punch onto his back.

Cullen crumpled.

Collapsed on the floor and struggling for breath, Cullen knew that he held the lives of the passengers in his hands. And although he would fight with everything for their survival, it wasn't looking good.

He was, after all, the last line of defence against Deep's destructive plan.

Or so he thought.

46

Deep was too busy glorying in his apparent defeat of Paul Cullen to notice Karl enter through the open cab doorway.

'Boss.'

Deep turned around, surprised, right into the oncoming punch. The blow from the larger man knocked him out cold, and he fell down hard onto the cab floor.

'I was always going to come back,' Karl said, gazing down on Deep's unconscious body.

Cullen hauled himself to his feet and grasped for the phone, exchanging a thank you glance with Karl, who had his knee on Deep's back, just as a precaution.

'Thomas, are you still there?' he said, the world wobbling slightly from Deep's blows.

There was no answer.

And no phone signal.

47

'Your phone,' Cullen said to Karl, is there any phone signal?

Karl took a look. 'No,' he said. 'Nothing.'

'Damn.' Cullen glared at the top icons on his phone screen, willing the reception to return.

What a time to lose connection!

He looked across at Deep, who was still motionless on the floor. It was as if, even incapacitated, he was still holding sway.

In desperation, Cullen began to stalk around the cab, holding the phone as high as he could, but it didn't make any difference.

Karl looked concerned. 'Before Deep arrived, did you manage to get anything from the driver?'

'Yes,' Cullen confirmed, finally giving up on the phone for now, and focusing instead on the only other alternative.

'Did he tell you how to stop the train?'

'He did,' Cullen said, looking at the panel in front of him as the train sped on, closer and closer to the bridge. 'He ran through it all with me.' Cullen thought hard about what

Thomas had said - which buttons, in what order. There were several steps. His finger hovered over a large blue button on the left hand side of the console.

He needed to be sure...

Eyes closed, fingers pinching the bridge of his nose, he tried to replay the conversation that had happened just a matter of minutes ago. Although to be fair, in between he had received a number of hard blows to his body, which was enough to affect anyone's memory.

'Big blue button on the left,' Cullen recited, 'then smaller blue button half-way down in the centre, and then red button on the right, which will disengage the autopilot and revert to manual.'

Cullen opened his eyes, and looked back at Karl. 'I think I've got it.'

'Go for it,' the bodyguard said. 'You've got this.'

Cullen turned back to the console and exhaled. He just hoped that he'd remembered it correctly. Pressing the wrong buttons, or the right buttons in the wrong order, might not necessarily cause any problems, but it certainly wouldn't stop them from careering off the track in just a few minutes' time. And if he hadn't managed to retrieve the correct procedure from his memory banks by now, there wasn't much hope of remembering it at all.

'I'm doing it,' Cullen said. With a slightly shaking hand, he depressed the big blue button, then moved his fingers across to the smaller one, and finally hit the red button.

It was only a matter of milliseconds before the display registered, but it felt like a lifetime.

AUTOPILOT DISENGAGED.

Cullen allowed himself a smile of relief. But the job was only half done.

'You did it!' Karl shouted.

'Not yet,' Cullen replied, retaining his concentration. 'Now I've got to remember how to stop this thing.'

'The big red button marked emergency stop?'

Cullen laughed at his stupidity as he reached for the stop button.

Nothing happened.

Karl looked in horror at Cullen. 'What the?'

The train sped on.

'I don't understand,' Karl said. 'Why aren't we slowing?'

Cullen stood rooted to the spot, utterly confused. 'I don't know...I'm not sure...I think...'

The answer was almost there, he knew it, but rising panic was blocking Cullen's thought process. 'Twice!' Cullen shouted at last, Thomas's words finally coming back to him like a light illuminating a pitch dark room, 'you have to hit it twice!'

Elation burst through as Cullen smacked the button like he was playing whack-a-mole at the funfair.

The effect was immediate.

'We're slowing!' Karl shouted, 'you did it! You did it!'

Cullen almost didn't dare to believe it, but Karl was right - the train was slowing, you could hear the emergency brakes squeezing the life out of the locomotive's once unstoppable momentum.

Cullen looked at his watch. 'We were five minutes until the bridge,' he said, leaning against the console, suddenly quite breathless. 'But that was with us travelling at eighty.'

'You've saved us all,' Karl said. 'You're a hero.'

Cullen didn't even hear him; he was looking at his phone.

The signal was back and Thomas Wellens was calling through.

48

'I'm sorry, Paul, I really am,' Maggie Ferguson said, as she addressed him across her desk first thing on Monday morning, back at British Transport Police Headquarters in North London. 'I really should have been more diligent in my checks before assigning you to this.'

'It's okay,' Cullen replied, downplaying his true feelings about the matter. 'No-one could have predicted what happened.'

Yes, he did harbour a little resentment at Maggie Ferguson's all too willingness to jump to powerful people, but there was another way of looking at what had taken place; a fact that was impossible to dismiss.

Without him, many innocent people would now be dead.

'I suppose it's actually good fortune that you were on the train,' she said, reading Cullen's mind. 'Otherwise we'd have an incredibly tragic incident on our hands - one of the most devastating rail disasters this country has ever seen.'

'Maybe me being there was meant to be,' Cullen conceded.

'Maybe. What you did, and the way you did it, also reflects very well on the British Transport Police. The Mayor is extremely happy with us. In fact, I've rarely seen him so delighted.'

Cullen smiled tightly as he shook his head.

Maggie Ferguson - always the politician.

'But the most important thing,' Maggie added, recognising Cullen's reaction, 'is that you're safe and well.'

'I live to fight another day,' Cullen quipped. 'But maybe I'll stay away from billionaires for the time being...actually maybe forever.'

'I think that's a very sensible idea,' Maggie said, mustering a smile. 'Not that Daniel Deep will be around to bother you any longer.'

'Quite.'

Daniel Deep was in custody, charged with attempted murder.

Bail had been refused because he was a flight risk.

'He would have been facing a very lengthly sentence,' she said, 'in ordinary circumstances.'

'Yes. I suppose a death sentence is more than enough,' Cullen stated. 'He gets to live out his final months at her Majesty's Pleasure. Not what he had in mind.'

Maggie nodded. 'A rather inauspicious end.'

'I meant to say,' Cullen said. 'The date of Philip's funeral has been confirmed. It's a week today. I assume the time off won't be a problem?'

'Of course not,' she said.

'Thank you.'

'My pleasure. If there's nothing else, Paul, I'll let you go. I'm sure there's plenty for you to catch up on.'

Cullen thought about the last time he had come to see Maggie. He'd been about to announce his resignation.

But that was before...

'Thank you, Ma'am.'

49

Grey skies hung low over the small church and cemetery in Wigan as Detective Chief Inspector Paul Cullen stood before the mourners, gathered to bid farewell to his childhood friend, Philip Sullivan.

The church was full to bursting, and filled with the scent of flowers. Cullen had been in reflective mood all that morning, his thoughts consumed by memories of his friend.

He had known the rugby player since they were children, growing up together in the same small town. They had been through everything together, and Cullen couldn't believe that he was now standing at his funeral, gazing down at Philip's coffin.

'Philip was a good man,' Cullen began the eulogy, his voice thick with emotion. 'We grew up together in this town. He was always the first to lend a hand to those in need, even if it meant putting his own needs aside. He was a true friend, always there for me, and for Sarah.'

Cullen's eyes scanned the congregation, taking in the somber faces of Philip's family and friends. He saw the tears on their cheeks, and felt a pang in his heart. Philip had been taken too soon, and it was a loss that would be felt by many.

'He was a man of great courage,' Cullen continued. 'On and off the rugby field. He fought his illness with everything he had, refusing to let it defeat him. And although, ultimately, it did take its toll, Philip, I believe, did come out victorious.'

Cullen talked some more of his friend's accomplishments on the rugby field, about his bravery and his determination. As he spoke, his mind was flooded with memories of the man, the sound of his laughter, the strength of his spirit. He remembered the times they had shared, the victories they had won, the challenges they had faced together.

But he also remembered the pain that his friend had gone through, the loss of memory, the confusion, the helplessness.

Cullen's voice finally broke as he approached the eulogy's final paragraph, and he took a deep breath before continuing. 'Philip was more than just a friend to me. He was family. And even though he's gone, he will always be a part of me and Sarah, and all who had the pleasure of knowing him. Rest in peace, my friend.'

Cullen returned to his seat, hugging Sarah close to him as the service continued.

As the service came to a close, Cullen felt a deep sadness wash over him. He couldn't help but think about his own mortality, about the fragility of life, about the inevitability of death and loss. He knew that he would never forget his friend, that his memory would always be with him, but he also knew that life would never be the same again.

As he left the church, Cullen felt a sense of determination take hold. He knew that he had to do something to honour Philip's memory, to make a difference in the fight against dementia. He would do whatever it took to make sure that no one else had to suffer the way his friend had.

And so, as he walked away, Cullen felt a renewed sense of purpose. He knew that his friend's legacy would live on through him, and that he would do everything in his power to make sure that his friend's death was not in vain.

50

Curtis Chesterfield couldn't quite believe his eyes, sitting there in his living room, newspaper in hand.

Daniel Deep remanded in custody.

He chuckled to himself as he read the words again. They were there in black and white, front page of the newspaper he had just picked up from the store.

Things were looking up.

Curtis had come clean to his wife Cindy about his gambling problem; the loses he had incurred and debts he had hid for so long.

It had been a painful, raw conversation and proceeding few days. But it had started to improve. She believed his promises; that he had not gambled in weeks now, and that he had sought help from an online self-help group.

It would take time of course to fully regain her trust, he recognised that, but he was there for the long haul.

Curtis pondered on the implications of Daniel Deep's arrest. Maybe it would make it harder to ever get justice for

Hope, if the one guy who could make a difference was in jail in England.

He broke out into a painful cough, not for the first time that day. The bouts would last anything from a few seconds up to several minutes. The cough felt deep, its genesis right from his core, and although the doctors hadn't found anything seriously wrong, it worried him.

It will take time, they said, for your system to settle down after your exposure.

The night of the derailment. The dreams of explosion, fire and nose-singeing stench had lingered for weeks, and were only now becoming less frequent.

Curtis heard someone outside the door, and assumed it was Cindy returning from her shopping trip, fiddling with her keys and rearranging bags so she could enter the house.

But then there was a knock.

Curtis rose from his chair to open the door.

To his great surprise, he found an unexpected guest waiting for him on the other side.

'Curtis,' Professor Brody said, standing there with a broad grin on his face.

'Professor,' Curtis replied, confused by the unannounced arrival. 'What are you doing here?'

'I come bearing gifts,' he said. He passed an envelope to Curtis. 'Go on,' he prompted, as Curtis held the item. 'Open it.'

Curtis did as he was told, revealing the contract signed by Daniel Deep at Laggan Castle. His eyes widened as he realised what he was reading.

'You got Daniel Deep to agree to this?'

'Sure did,' Brody smiled. 'Just before he was locked up for

being the criminal that he undoubtedly is. Now how about you invite me in?' He held up some beers that he'd been holding by his side. 'I've got the drinks and the signed contract, so let's get down to business.'

PAUL CULLEN WILL RETURN IN "MAY DAY"

Visit Paul's website to find out more about his writing:

www.paulpilkington.com

You can also follow Paul on Amazon via his profile, to be notified of new releases (just click on the follow button):

ACKNOWLEDGMENTS

I hope you enjoyed Deep Sleeper. Thank you for your continued support with my writing. It means a lot to me that for the past twelve years I have been able to connect with thousands of people from across the world who have read my books. I will never take it for granted.

Best wishes,

Paul

ABOUT THE AUTHOR

Paul Pilkington is a British author of mystery, suspense and thriller novels. He is best known for his Emma Holden Suspense Mystery series, which follows the story of a young actress named Emma Holden who is thrown into a world of danger and intrigue after the sudden disappearance of her fiancé. Paul has also written several best-selling standalone novels, including For Your Own Protection and Someone to Save You, as well as the Detective Paul Cullen mystery series.

Paul's writing style is fast-paced, suspenseful, and character-driven. His novels explore complex themes and issues, such as love, loss, family, and redemption.

Printed in Great Britain
by Amazon

37489206R00151